Bill Scott

THE LADDER PROJECT

Copyright © 2022 by Bill Scott

ISBN: 979-8-88653-010-0

Melange Books, LLC
White Bear Lake, MN 55110
www.melange-books.com

Published in the United States of America.

Cover Design by Ashley Redbird Designs

Dedicated to Mrs. Durr, my 4th grade arithmetic teacher, because she taught me how to learn.

Chapter One
1968

The floor looks different from down here, he thought as he strained to focus on a wood-grained pattern spanning a horizontal landscape. It appeared to end far away where he imagined a pinhole of light racing towards him at one-thousand miles-per-hour. He made no attempt to move out of its way. He could not have moved even if he had wanted. It was as if plastic wrap had been slammed down over his body and pinned him to the floor. The tunnel he envisioned stopped directly beneath an antique cuckoo clock—a grotesque Salvador Dali creation with a dying bird and a missing hour-hand.

Mark Todd lay motionless for a time. He had the urge to go back to sleep, but the buzzing in his brain mimicked a noisy alarm clock without a snooze button.

In addition to a torrent of confusion, a spectacular show of brightly colored lights accompanied a persistent throbbing that radiated shards of lightning throughout his skull. He tried to focus on a point at the end of his nose. It looked huge and appeared to be decorated with red paint like that of a circus clown.

Immediately before the lights went out, he remembered opening the door to his apartment and placing his keys on a small, walnut table—one of the remaining heirlooms he had decided to keep after his parents disappeared. What once was a table lay thoroughly disassembled in front of him. He reached up and grasped the doorframe and, with a great deal of effort, pulled himself into a standing position.

Fumbling around in his left-rear pocket, he pulled out a handkerchief and attempted to wipe the blood from his face. It came off in pieces, telling him whoever left him in such a disorganized heap must have vacated the premises long before he regained consciousness.

He groped his way to the far end of the living room and into the kitchen where he located a tall, green bottle resting on the kitchen sink. Pouring a generous amount of J&B into a short glass, he added an inch or two of tap water and slammed it down, resulting in a familiar seizure of coughing and wheezing that accompanied it.

"Shit, how can anybody drink this crap?" He shuddered. The first slug of scotch always gave him the willies...the way castor oil affected him when his mother tried to force it through his clamped jaws. Immediately, he poured a second one.

Making his way to the couch, he fumbled with the telephone dial several times before managing to generate a number in a format that Ma Bell recognized. The infernal buzzing of the phone terminated with a groggy but familiar voice on the other end of the line.

"Harry here," —— "Hello? Hello?"

"Harry...it's Mark," the man said. "I need you to come to my apartment immediately."

Harry was a pain in the ass. Mark hated having a babysitter, but Walter had insisted on providing him with a nannie, and he had chosen Harry for that task.

"What's up, big fella?" he asked.

"Somebody rearranged my scalp when I got home."

"Why doesn't that surprise me?" Harry mumbled in response. "I've been meaning to bring you up-to-date on the perils of jealous husbands."

Mark waved his left index finger around in front of his eyes, trying to focus on the tiny swirls that formed his fingerprint. "Say, what time is it anyway?"

"Are you okay?"

"I think so——a little disoriented, perhaps."

"It's two in the morning, for Christ sakes, can't it wait?"

"Listen you insensitive weasel," Mark shouted. "I need your help, and I need it right now!"

"Awright, awright," he said. "I'll be there in fifteen minutes."

Mark took a quick look around the apartment and found everything in order, everything but his aching body that is. He pulled a tray of ice cubes out of the Frigidaire and made an ice pack out of an old dishrag. Two cubes escaped and skittered across the floor, but Mark paid no mind and made his way back to the living room, collapsed on the sofa and continued to collect his thoughts.

In a short time, there was a familiar knock on the door. Two knocks, a pause, followed by three knocks—Harry Swanson's trademark.

"Come in," Mark said, loud enough for any normal human being to hear. But Harry, being abnormal in Mark's estimation, knocked a second time.

"Goddamit," Mark cursed as he struggled to rise from the

sofa. Before he had circumvented the coffee table, Harry was standing in the room.

"Doggies, Jethro," Harry remarked, imitating Jed Clampett from an episode of the Beverly Hillbillies, "you look like you been sorting wildcats in a burnin' hayloft."

Mark tossed him a look of disgust, struggled back to the couch, and plopped himself down again. He reapplied the hastily made ice pack to his forehead. Two additional cubes escaped, skittered across the floor, and bounced off the wall.

"Who did it?" Harry asked.

"Damned if I know," Mark replied. "The last thing I remember is dropping my keys on the table by the door."

Mark took another sip of his drink, pointed to the bar, and said, "You want one?"

"Pity," Harry said, kicking ice cubes out of his path and making a beeline for the scotch.

"Did you call Walter?" Harry shouted from the kitchen.

"And tell him what?"

"You wuz robbed?"

"Nothing's missing as far as I can tell, and I don't think Walter would be interested in a fucked-up robbery."

Harry took a seat in the chair in front of the coffee table. Setting his drink down, he retrieved a cigarette from a partially squashed pack of Lucky's. Fumbling around in his pocket, he produced a well-worn, World War II Zippo, ignited it, lit the Lucky, and leaned back blowing smoke making a circle above his head.

"What's the plan?" he asked.

"We need to get to the lab ASAP."

"Now?"

"Right fuckin' now."

"You don't wanna call Walter first?"

"No, I *do not* wanna call Walter, not until we check on a few things first.

"Harry, call security and give 'em a heads up," Mark ordered. "Tell 'em to go to a medium-alert state until we get there. I'll clean up and we'll get moving."

"Roger that," Harry said and picked up the phone to make the call.

The main gate of Barksdale Air Force Base was located along Airline Drive. It was manned by a young Air Force second lieutenant and three lesser-ranked APs armed with M-14s.

Carpet-bombing of North Vietnam was cranking up into high gear. At least one bomb-laden, B-52 Stratofortress took off from Barksdale every hour around the clock. Even a squirrel was expected to show ID before making it through any of the gates.

The officer on duty gave Mark the customary salute and assured him that after a thorough investigation they had uncovered no evidence of an attempted entry into the lab, and nothing unusual had taken place.

"Don't salute me, you idiot. Do you see any bars on my shoulders?" *God, I hate these gung-ho military idiots,* he thought.

"No, sir," the lieutenant replied, dropping his salute and re-assuming parade rest at the entrance to the guardhouse.

After Mark and Harry had signed the logbook, Harry drove to the building where the lab was located, parked in his assigned parking space, and they both exited the vehicle. Mark entered his security code into a keypad, and they entered the building.

At four in the morning, the lab was devoid of PhDs running around in their white coats. They wouldn't start filtering in until around six.

Half the lab was occupied by an environmentally controlled computer room. A recently acquired IBM System/360 was busily running overnight calculations. Twenty-one tape drives spun silently, like the gears of some monstrous mechanical apparatus contemplating the end of the world. Harry made a detour to the printer room to search through recent reports, looking for anything with their name on it.

"Nada," he said as he entered the cubicle where Mark was sitting.

"Find out what time Langstrum will come in today."

"He usually gets here around eight," Harry replied. "You want me to call him?"

"Let him sleep... he's gonna need it. Get the conference room set up for a meeting. I need an update on yesterday's progress."

* * *

Skimming through the reports, Mark found the overnight printouts not much different from the day before, and the day before that—one depressing failure after another. Not since 1953, when biologists Watson and Crick conceived of the *double helix* with rungs connecting two strands to form a molecule of DNA, had any serious advances been made in their research. It was apparent to Mark that his Einsteins weren't about to disappoint him by breaking the tedious trend.

Unlocking the code to life's greatest mysteries had confounded the largest single collection of assembled scientific researchers since the *Manhattan Project*. No less urgent, success on *The Ladder Project* depended on the same magnitude of scientific breakthroughs. It had become an obsession of the CIA: if the Russians succeeded in being first in the creation of artificial life, they would surely attempt to use it to gain world domination. Dr. Langstrum was the 'you're it' character in the game of biogenetic tag.

Peter Langstrum was a graduate of MIT and was the best choice the US government could come up with to manage the scientists in *The Ladder Project,* much as Oppenheimer had done the same in the Manhattan Project. Wanting someone capable of coming up with fresh ideas, and his thesis, "Single-Molecule Detection and DNA Sequencing by Synthesis", caught the attention of the director of the CIA, and he was hired before he completed his post-doc.

In his paper, Peter had concluded the success of creating synthetic organisms depended upon the ability to rearrange polynucleotide chains in such a way as to expedite the process of injecting DNA molecules into bacterial cells.

Langstrum was assisted by a team of twenty more molecular biology specialists, housed in a building inside Barksdale Air Force Base, just outside of Shreveport, in Bossier City, Louisiana.

Mark's opinion of Langstrum was that he was an anally retentive asshole with a personality akin to a pile of dog shit. No matter. He was also certain Langstrum felt the same about him. Like Leslie R. Groves who was in charge of the *Manhattan Project*, Mark Todd knew he was hated and despised by the teams assigned under Langstrum. He could care less. His management style was more like that of George S. Patton who expected to be treated as an unquestionable god, whereas Oppenheimer was a captivating individual and a charismatic figure that could easily draw people's attention and inter-est——a quality he found missing in Langstrum.

Growing up in Massachusetts on Rachel Cove in the forties, Mark Todd had been blessed with wealthy parents and a lavish lifestyle. His family and everyone who they associated with were incurable, liberal democrats.

His parents were crushed when Eisenhower beat Adlai Stevenson in the '52 presidential election. When Ike prevailed again in '56, they rolled in their virtual graves.

But when one of their own bested Nixon in 1960, they were vindicated at last, and the mumbling and grumbling gave way to wild, drunken orgies that seemed to go on forever.

Mark, on the other hand, always detested politics and ran from political discussions whenever they came up. Nevertheless, his parent's wealth and political connections bought his way into a world-class education and went on to serve him well during the early days of his career.

After graduating from high school, Cambridge, Massachusetts, became his home. He rarely saw his parents much after that. One day at the end of his senior year at MIT, during a class, out of the blue, the dean called him to his office and told him his parents had gone missing somewhere out in the Atlantic, east of Nahant. Neither the boat nor his parents were ever recovered.

He gave them an extravagant memorial that drew the elite who's-who from all around the New England area. The president's brother Teddy gave the eulogy and the president himself sent a wreath that would rival first prize at the Kentucky Derby. In the spring, Mark became one of the few millionaires to graduate from MIT. No relatives showed up to help mark the auspicious occasion.

After that, Mark stayed on at the university for two more years to get his engineering degree, and another four to receive his doctorate. His thesis was entitled, *DNA Evolution and Replication of Proteins and Genes.*

An old friend of the family landed him a civilian job with

the CIA, where he became intensely interested in project management. This led to him being assigned as Project Manager to *The Ladder Project*.

Mark Todd never married. The reason wasn't that he didn't care for women, he just didn't care for them very long. Not much of a drinker, he satisfied his urges by making his rounds to the bars in Cambridge and picking up the occasional coed who found him interesting enough for a one-night stand. There was a new supply of women every fall, and he would pick through them like one would search for pecans in a canister containing mostly peanuts. He rarely went out with a woman more than once. Never receiving love from his own mother and father, growing up as a strange sort of orphan, he never got lonely and the thought of starting a family was foreign to him. He had known families for sure, but he never entertained the idea of having one himself.

Mark did have at least one romance that started off with promise, but the moment she told him she planned on becoming the mother of at least three, he avoided her as one would avoid a stack of radioactive plutonium. He could not fathom being a father.

The mechanism by which organisms maintain their genomic integrity is through a process called *DNA repair*. This process is closely related to evolution. The threat to genomic integrity is what keeps evolution cooking. If not, things would remain pretty much as they were 580 million years ago. In fact, without threats to the integrity of the genome, we would probably still be nothing more than single-cell organisms swimming around in a sea of salt water—or maybe we wouldn't *be* at all.

In short, the continuation of life and the primary reason that accounts for us having two legs, two eyes, and one nose, is the product of genomes fighting off evil forces from which they are constantly under attack.

A virus cannot replicate itself unless it can find its way into a living cell. It replicates itself by attaching itself to a cell wall, injects itself into the host's cell, hijacks it, and begins the replication process. The new viruses burst out of the cell, killing it in the process, and goes on to infect and destroy new cells.

'T cells' from the immune system are constantly in search of these infections. If a 'T cell' identifies an infected cell, it kills it, and the replication process is terminated, but some viruses have the ability to avoid detection and go about the replication process unchallenged. It takes time for the immune system to recognize the virus and be able to detect its presence. The longer the virus goes undetected, the greater the damage it causes.

* * *

It's ironic that violence is responsible for our being, for our very existence, and as history keeps demonstrating—for our undoing. *He who lives by the sword*, etcetera, etcetera. Life is war at the microscopic level. It sustains itself through one violent conflict after another, both large and small, inside and out.

Sun Tzu said: "In conflict, direct confrontation will lead to engagement and surprise will lead to victory. Those who are skilled in producing surprise will win."

Every day of our lives, whether sleeping or awake, epic wars are ongoing just beneath our skin.

* * *

Molecular biology was gaining in popularity while Mark was working on his thesis—its major aim being, the comparison of entire genomes of different species. How does a cow differ from a buffalo, a deer from a gazelle, or a horse from an elephant? The answers lay in the comparison of the genomes, and molecular biologists did that by meticulously examining the gene sequence of similar organisms.

It's much like *code-breaking*. By breaking a code, we can decipher the true meaning of a complete message. The number of times a letter appears in a coded message gives us a clue as to what the letter translates to. More guesses must be made, which results in backtracking to eliminate and validate previous assumptions.

One letter transposed to another letter is simply a single step in the process. We have to go on to decipher complete words, sentences and paragraphs before the message has meaning. Breaking the code of the Creator is what it's all about.

Mark had always been fascinated with the idea of the universe being created when an infinitesimal speck exploded and spewed clouds of dust and gas into a void. And that microscopic speck somehow created a universe of unimaginable size? Imagining how a dot infinitely small, evolved to a universe unimaginably large, made him ponder as to just how small *is* small, and just how large *is* large? What started the process and when will it end? Which came first, life or DNA?

When Walter offered Mark the position of being the leader of a group of researchers seeking the origin of life, he jumped at the chance. Working on a project with an unlimited budget came with its advantages. The idea of overseeing a group destined to create the first life form to survive outside of Earth's environment was irresistible.

But then, as one failure after another piled up, he began to lose interests. He started to doubt whether the project could ever be finished. Had he worked his way into a prison from which there was no escape, both scientifically and physically?

Thirty minutes before the meeting, he decided to call Walter and bring him up to date.

The CIA operated in a three-tier management structure. The top tier was the Director of the CIA. The second tier served as a liaison between the top tier and the third and monitored the progress of orders or directives that came down from the Director himself.

Mark's job at the bottom tier included monitoring and reporting the progress of the scientists to the second tier who would pass the information along to the Director. Walter was his second-tier manager.

Mark worked in the sewers of the CIA—shit rolls downhill and he caught his share. Walter picked up the phone on the second ring.

"Speak," he said.

Forget it, Mark thought. *I'm used to this by now.*

"Walter, it's Mark," he said.

"Have good news for a change?"

"Somebody tried to bash my brains in when I walked into my apartment last night."

"Say, that *is* good news. Maybe it reorganized some neurons so we can get a decent day's work out of you?"

"If I had any sense, I'd be making roach spray for Dow Chemical," Mark countered.

"Did they catch the guy? I'd like to offer him your job."

"What makes you think it was a guy?"

"Well, there's that," he laughed. "And the package?"

"It's here in the lab with me."

"Make sure it stays there."

What kind of idiot does he take me for? Mark thought. *Does he think I wear the damn thing around my neck?*

"Look, Walter. I just wanted to let you know what happened before it gets back to you."

"You okay?"

"If you discount this lump on the top of my head, and the lighting strikes in it...I guess I'll make it alright."

"You take care of that lump, son. It could have a brain in it."

"Funny," Mark said. "Nothing new...I'll call you later."

The project manager hung up the phone just as Harry walked into his cubicle.

"Langstrum just arrived. He needs five minutes to clear his desk."

"Put a pot of coffee on. We're gonna need it," Mark ordered.

The meager conference room bore no resemblance to the usual ones seen in block-buster type, military movies. It looked more like the conference room in *Get Smart*, minus the cone of silence.

Peter Langstrum sat across the small table, thumbing through his notes. He wore glasses much too large for his face. It gave him the appearance of a bug-eyed goldfish. He looked up when his boss entered the room.

"Dr. Langstrum," Mark said, "the reports on my desk don't give me cause for celebration. I hope you have better news for me."

The little man removed his glasses, rubbed the indentions they made in his nose, wiped his spectacles on his sleeve, and repositioned them on his head.

"I'm sorry, Mark—I, I don't..."

Mark Todd set his jaw and gritted his teeth.

"Jesus, what happened to you?" Langstrum was staring at the bump on Mark's head.

"I was bobbing for apples in the toilet and the lid hit me. Don't change the subject," he warned. "The United States government fully expects to get their money's worth. You Einsteins have been working on this project for twenty-three months and produced nothing of value."

Langstrum's eyes dropped to his hands.

"Look, Peter. I know you and your team have been burning the midnight oil. Maybe it's time to back-off and try a new approach."

"But we're getting *so* close."

"That's what you said during our last little get-together. But tell me, are you making any progress?"

"At least we've identified thousands of possibilities that don't work. That's what it's all about. Edison failed thousands of times before he invented the incandescent light bulb, you know."

"Yeah, and if you'd been running the show, we'd still be working by candlelight."

"That was uncalled for, Mark."

"Two years without success is uncalled for, Peter."

"Well—you want me to quit?"

"No, goddamnit, I want you to *finish*."

Peter went into his imitation of a poor whipped puppy.

Mark softened his demeanor and tried to appeal to Langstrum's sensitivity. "Look, Peter. I'm not trying to give you a hard time. Sometimes you work on a project for so long there comes a time when you need to go back to the start and retrace your steps. So, just take a short break to organize your thoughts and let's start over from the beginning."

Langstrum left the table and poured himself a cup of coffee. When he retook his seat, he appeared to be more relaxed.

"Look, Mark," he began. "Let's review. As you know,

biotechnology can be compared to an older interaction with nature—for example gardening, which relies heavily on pruning and grafting.

"Gene-by-gene biotechnology constantly comes up with the problem that living organisms tend to plough through the furrows so-to-speak," Peter made a plowing motion with his hands, "despite all of our efforts to control them.

"The pruning part of our work involves eliminating proclivities that might be useful to a wild organism but drain the energy and metabolic effort away from the task at hand. The grafting part is adding new characteristics from elsewhere to the well-trained root stock.

"Our steps began by carefully determining the sequence of the total genomic DNA, about a million base-pairs of a simple bacterium called *Mycoplasma mycoides*. Overlapping segments of the complete sequence were then synthesized in the lab by the ordered stitching together of the four DNA bases."

"So, you were successful in synthesizing the sequence of the total genomic DNA. I don't see a problem here," Mark said, shaking his head.

"There isn't one to that point. We went on to clone and assemble the segments of the copied sequence in yeast cells..."

Langstrum was interrupted by Harry entering the room.

"The Provost Marshall wants to see you in the hall," Harry reported.

"We'll continue this conversation later," Mark said to Langstrum. "I think I'd better see to this new development. You think about what I said," he added, pointing his finger in Peter's face.

Leaving the conference area and making his way down the hall, he ran into a warrant officer of about thirty years of age, wearing military fatigues and armed to the teeth.

"How can I help you?" Mark asked.

"I understand you experienced a break-in last night," the officer said.

"Not here," he assured him.

"At your home, right?"

Mark nodded in the affirmative.

"Why didn't you report the incident to the proper military authorities?"

"For what reason?" Mark replied. "Nothing was taken. It was probably just some local burglar looking for TVs and silverware."

"How can you be sure?"

"As I said, nothing was stolen. I assumed I surprised him, and the only way out was through me."

"Nevertheless, Mr. Todd, I've been ordered to launch an investigation. Could I trouble you for the keys to your apartment?"

Mark fished in his pocket, removed his apartment key from a steel ring and handed it to the Warrant Officer.

"Base housing has been arranged for you at Bachelor Officer's Quarters. Your clothes and personal items will be delivered there. You need to come with me. We'll talk on the way."

Mark followed the warrant officer out of the building, taking his place in the passenger's seat of the Provost Marshall's car.

"Mr. Todd, we have reason to believe an operative of a foreign power has targeted you."

"You mean...following me around?"

"I think she was in your apartment when you got home last night."

Chapter Two

"She? How do you know it was a she? I don't have anything there that anyone would want."

"Just the same, we can't let you go back there. We're going to do a full sweep of the apartment and remove everything that belongs to you. As far as the world's concerned, you don't live there anymore."

"But what about my mail, the bills?"

"They'll be forwarded to headquarters and delivered to your room at the BOQ. No one must know where you live."

The Provost Marshall escorted Mark to his new quarters, retrieved the key to his room from the office, and led him to it.

"We feel it would be in the country's best interest if you didn't leave the base until further notice. The same is true for your team. *No one* leaves the base until CID gives me an okay."

"Now, now wait just a damn minute. I have a personal life, you know," Mark argued.

"Not anymore you don't, Mr. Todd," the Warrant Officer announced in an authoritative manner. "You may go anywhere on the base as long as you're accompanied by an escort.

Someone will pick you up when you're ready to go to work and bring you back here to sleep."

He shoved a card into Mark's hand. "If you need to go anywhere on base at any other time, call this number and we'll send a driver."

"What am I, a prisoner?" Mark complained.

"That's exactly what you are, Mr. Todd. Now, if you're ready to go back to your office, I'll have someone drive you there."

Mark Todd sat on a green, vinyl covered sofa, the kind he'd remembered sitting on in a dentist's office twenty years before. He stared at an ancient Motorola TV with rabbit ears for a crown and aluminum wrap to enhance its reception. The room was small, a lot smaller that the comfortable townhouse he had leased near to the base. It had brown, shabby curtains, a bed and next to it a stained bedside table, a telephone, a walk-in closet, a small kitchen, a refrigerator, a stove, and off to the side a tiny bathroom/shower... All in all it was barely larger than a room one might find in a cheap motel that offered monthly rates for transit workers. In Mark's view, it was deplorable to say the least.

"I'd suggest you get accustomed to your new surroundings, Mr. Todd. You may experience restrictive activity for some time."

Todd was only half listening. Both guilt and fear washed over him like a tidal wave.

"A man will be stationed in the lobby during the daytime while you're here and at your office while you're there." The Warrant Officer walked out of the room and closed the door, leaving Mark to contemplate the current situation.

Was I a suspect? he thought. *Why such harsh treatment?* He immediately picked up the phone and dialed Walter's number.

"Speak," his superior answered.

"Walter, what the hell's going on here? How come I'm being treated like a criminal?"

"Are you a criminal?" Walter said.

"Hell no, you know damned well I would *never* do anything to jeopardize our work."

"You already have," he shot back. "You know that female you picked up at the Orbit Lounge last week?"

"Vaguely..."

"We think she's the one that put your lights out."

"Hell, I don't even know her, Walter. It was just a one-night stand, for God's sakes. You can't expect me to live here like a monk."

"You need a reality check, Mark. You're in charge of the most crucial operation since the Manhattan Project. We'll see about getting you a professional from time to time. But for the time being ..."

"A prostitute?" Mark interrupted, showing a heightened sense of amazement.

"It's your choice, buddy. We can arrange a lady friend for you, or you can do without. Look, I gotta run. Get your ass back to work and put the spurs to your team. The Director is losing his patience."

Walter hung up the phone. Mark sat there trying to evaluate his situation. *This is unbelievable*, he thought. *But I'll be damned if I can figure out a solution*. He went downstairs and met his escort to take him back to the lab.

The incident knocked the stuffing out of him. Immediately, he regretted raking Langstrum over the coals. Now he understood the true meaning of humiliation. He hadn't been taking his responsibilities seriously. He knew that now. Walter was correct about one thing. He desperately needed a reality check.

When he returned to the lab, Langstrum had left a note on his desk.

I suggest, at our next meeting, we get the entire team together. We'll be ready when you are...Peter

The tiny conference room was far too small to assemble the entire team, so the meeting was set to be held in one of the labs for a roundtable discussion with Mark officiating. It took an hour for all of the participants to get to a stopping place in their work.

Mark wondered if Harry Swanson had anything to do with his predicament. He had never felt comfortable around that bastard and now he liked him even less. He also wondered if Walter's reason for hiring Harry was to keep tabs on him. Then it dawned on him just how isolated he had allowed himself to become. He had suspected that Harry had been prying into his private affairs more than usual and he didn't like it one bit. He made a mental note to distance himself from the man and keep future conversations isolated to those that were necessary, and strictly business in nature.

He decided he needed to get more involved in the project. In the past few months, he had allowed his attitude to degrade tremendously. He had even entertained the idea of asking Walter to find a replacement, but now that he felt the rug sliding out from under him, he feared that decision was in danger of being made for him.

Twenty-three months of acting like a tyrant hadn't produced any results. Maybe he needed a new approach. Maybe he needed to win over the friendship of his staff instead. He would start by being more empathetic to their struggles. He would start building their confidence in him with this meeting.

No more Mr. Asshole. How could it hurt?

When Mark entered the room, twenty excited geneticists

were arguing among themselves. It was apparent Langstrum had kicked over a hornet's nest and each of them had experienced a painful sting.

"Good afternoon, people," Todd began. "Time is short, and I won't keep you away from your work any longer than necessary."

He pulled up a metal chair and positioned himself in full view of the entire group. Everyone started asking questions at once. He raised his hand, "Ladies...gentlemen—please. I have a few things to say, after which we can get on with an orderly discussion."

The room fell silent.

"For the past two years, you people have been working your butts off and I'd like you to know I appreciate it, and your government appreciates it. In addition, I'm sure Dr. Langstrum appreciates it as well."

Peter nodded in agreement.

"Up to this point, for the most part, you have been enjoying your freedom and individuality. Up until this moment, you have been isolated into groups, with each group communicating to other groups through Peter. However, as you may know, a recent event has taken place which compels us to begin working together as a single, well-coordinated team. The critical nature of our research has resulted in undesirable restrictions on all of us and we will all have to make adjustments to our individual freedoms and our lifestyles.

"For what it's worth, I'd like to make it clear, I wasn't consulted as to this change before it was announced. It came as a shock to me just as it was for each of you.

"Dr. Langstrum will continue to preside as your team-leader, and my responsibilities as the project leader will not change, with one exception—I will become an active member of the research group and assist Dr. Langstrum in his work."

Langstrum twisted in his chair.

"Let me assure you all, I have no intentions of interfering with Dr. Langstrum's duties in any way. As far as you're concerned, he's still the boss and my role at this level will be strictly of an advisory nature.

"One personal note, I know my reputation of being an unmitigated asshole clouds the environment..."

A few chuckles were heard from the gathering, however Mark managed to retain his serious demeanor.

"But that situation will end as of now. While my education may not be as extensive as Dr. Langstrum's, at the least, I hold a certificate from MIT equal to the credentials of fifty percent of the ladies and gentlemen seated in this room.

"Nevertheless, I feel I have let you down. I have behaved as a tyrant, and I have come to the opinion that my actions may have done more damage to this project than aided in its progress. For that, you have my sincere apology.

"As of now, my sharp tones and offensive behavior have come to an end. I regret my hard-assed attitude and encourage you to accept me as a working member of the team."

He paused for a moment to let his confession settle into the minds of the other scientists.

"Now, do any of you have any problems with this?"

Receiving no response, negative or otherwise, he went on. "Since there appear to be no objections, without further ado I will turn this meeting over to Dr. Langstrum."

Peter rose from his chair, thanked Mark for his remarks and assured him that he spoke for all in welcoming Mark into the active team of research geneticists.

He made it clear, rather than having twenty scientists

working independently, it was more like ten teams composed of two researchers each working in tandem. He suggested each team introduce themselves and provide a brief ten-minute overview as to what projects they were currently working on.

Mark Todd took a clean sheet of paper out of his notebook and began taking notes. The presentations went on for two hours, after which the meeting was adjourned, and Peter and Mark remained to go over Mark's notes.

"It appears to me that many of these teams are working on the same processes," Mark said.

"I've tried to manage it the best way I knew how under the circumstances, but as the orders stood, each team has been isolated from the other for security reasons," he said. "It hampered our ability in dozens of ways. We have discussed this in the past, but I had no choice and did the best I could. I think this new arrangement will make the research go faster and it happens to be the only good thing I can come up with at the moment.

"For Christ sakes, Mark. I don't know how the government gets anything done. I was speaking to a friend who works at the EPA and he told me that the office to save America's forests was located directly across from the office that lobbied to cut a great deal of it down. What's this country coming to?" It was a delivered as declarative statement.

"Well, since it appears we've all been sequestered for the duration, I suspect secrecy amongst the teams is no longer a necessary requirement."

"I'm getting a lot of resistance over this new directive, Mark."

"That's understandable, but it looks as if we don't have any say in the matter."

"I've even heard some grumblings about quitting."

"That's impossible, Peter. They may quit, but they won't be allowed to leave."

"So, it's true...what they're saying...we *are* prisoners here?"

"Yes, you could put it that way—in velvet chains."

"Christ all mighty," Peter exclaimed. "How can they do this?"

"I suppose they can do whatever they want. I've been forced out of my apartment and over to the BOQ, but I suspect they'll move us all into a segregated compound as soon as they can arrange to have one built, with the exception of those with families who have been given base housing already, but the restrictions for leaving the base still apply."

"That explains your sudden change of heart?"

"Hmmm...it's a bit more than that, but I suppose it was this new directive that pushed me over the edge."

"Do you think this new compound will have cells?" Peter scoffed.

"On the contrary, I suspect it will be a virtual paradise. They may imprison us, but there's no doubt they'll attempt to make up for our isolation by treating us as VIPs. I've already been offered prostitutes," he chuckled. "I think they'll go overboard to make us as comfortable as possible."

"We could sure use a new coffee machine," Peter joked.

"Now that will never happen," Mark said.

"Makes one wonder as to what we're actually doing here." Peter bit his lip and stared off into space.

"I have only the Manhattan Project to relate to. At times, I heard those guys were threatening to riot. Thank God we have air conditioning. Those poor bastards had to tough it out in the desert with fans."

"I heard Groves was an asshole too," Peter laughed. "No offense, Mark."

"None taken. Yeah, but he got the job done, didn't he?"

"Say, whatever happened to that old fart, anyway?"

"He continued on as the head of the atomic establishment until '47, then he headed up a special weapons project, retired, and became a VP at Sperry Rand."

"At least they didn't neutralize him."

"That's the only thought that keeps my spirits up," Mark chuckled. "Okay, let's get back to the problem at hand. We've got to solve this thing or our 'compound' will be turned into an ol' folk's home.

"Of all the groups that spoke, one stands out. Robinson and Walters were successful in synthesizing a highly accurate sequence of the total genomic DNA, correct?"

"That's right," Peter replied. "Using that as a template, they prepared a set of short DNA strands. We're calling them 'cassettes', each about one-thousand base-pairs long. They inserted the cassettes into yeast cells where the yeasts' own genetic machinery strung them together into a copy of the natural Mycoplasma mycoides genome."

"Well, what went wrong?"

"They had to find a way to transplant the 1.1 million base-pair long synthetic genome into cells of bacteria, and it had to be a closely related bacterial species, but distinct, to create what we would call a 'synthetic cell', although only the genome would be synthetic. Months of attempts at transplanting the synthetic genome have failed to yield living cells," he added.

Mark pondered over the problem for a few moments. "I think I can help you solve this problem, Peter. If not, we'll bring in someone who will.

"We need to assign two geneticists to repeat the process. There must be an explanation as to why they failed because, logically, it sounds correct. It could be one, tiny step they missed that would've made the experiment a success."

Both men agreed the events that occurred during the day had worn them to a frazzle. They decided to call it quits and get a fresh start in the morning. It was Mark's gut feeling that they should pare the project down to the basics and focus the combined efforts of the entire team on the successful transplantation of a synthetic genome that would result in the successful formation of a living cell. If they were able to do that, it would provide them with a platform for moving forward.

That evening, Mark left the lab with his notes in hand. After a simple dinner at the Officer's Club, his escort drove him back to the BOQ. He found his clothes and most of his personal belongings neatly stored away. His razor, toothbrush and shaving lotion were in the bathroom. He decided to push the envelope by testing his freedom.

Putting on his jogging pants, tennis shoes and a sweatshirt, he walked outside and began a jog around the base. A dark blue sedan kept a safe distance away, but the driver made no attempt to disguise his presence. The thunder of a departing B-52 Stratofortress broke the silence of an otherwise quiet evening. When he jogged across an open field, the car was right there waiting on the other side, parked at the curb.

Returning to his room, he took a leisurely shower and put on his pajamas. He reviewed his diary of the last two years until his eyes grew tired. The old black and white Motorola provided background noise. He made a mental note to pick up a small clock radio at the base commissary.

He had begun to get used to the revving up of the jet engines every hour or so while he was living at his apartment. It was merely a bit louder in his new surroundings.

The roar could be heard for ten miles in all directions. It had become known as the sound of security against the fear of retaliation by the dreaded Red Tide that was advancing across the Earth. At least here, no bombs were falling, Old Glory still waved, and everything was okay in *the Land of the Free and the Home of the Brave.* After a while, he switched off the television and climbed into bed.

Sleep didn't come easy. His mind was racing a million miles an hour. Finally, around 4:00 a.m. a dark veil of oblivion washed over him and rescued him from his mental anguish.

The following morning, when he arrived at work, yet another unpleasant surprise awaited him. One of their geneticists had committed suicide.

Harry Robinson's research assistant Diane Walters found his body hanging from the ceiling in his apartment. An overturned chair lay directly beneath him. She had made the gruesome discovery after he didn't show up for breakfast in the private mess hall where they took their meals. When it came time to leave for work, she decided to check and see if he had overslept.

Walters was understandably distraught and unable to provide the investigating officer with any information regarding the circumstances of his death. The chief investigator, a captain by the name of Peters, wrote in his report that he felt she had more information than she was willing to provide when he questioned her. Nevertheless, she was not suspected of any wrongdoing. All the evidence appeared to point to a cut and dried suicide.

Later that same day, Mark requested Dr. Walters to join him in his cubicle. She entered the room cautiously and set down in a chair opposite him. Taking a tissue from her lab coat, she dabbed her eyes, crumpled it in her hands and held it tightly in her lap.

"Do you feel like talking?" Mark asked Diane.

She nodded in an apathetic way.

Diane Walters was an attractive woman in her early thirties. She had acquired her master's degree in molecular biology from the University of Toronto, where she graduated with honors. The daughter of a well-to-do Canadian businessman and a woman of Chinese descent, she had her mother's features— short legs and light, clear, yellowish-skin—giving the hint that her ancestors probably came from the higher elevations in the Northern regions of China.

Her eyes were slanted in an attractive sort of way and shaped like almonds. Being somewhat thin in stature, her hair was straight, and the color of black shoe polish. It complimented her dark-brown eyes.

She acquired an H1B visa while working on her PhD defense, finished her post-doc at UT and then immigrated to California, where she had obtained a position in the Molecular Biology department of Caltech. On her 28th birthday, she took the oath and became a naturalized American citizen.

Never married, she seemed dedicated to her work. Mark didn't know her in social circles, but from the rumor-mill it got back to him she had left a young engineer in Pasadena with a broken heart. He wanted children, and she wanted the Nobel Prize. She jumped at the opportunity to join with her colleagues in the search for the origin of life.

On the staff since its beginnings, glancing over her dossier told Mark she was quite capable of doing the work for which she had been assigned. He offered to get her a soda, and she declined.

"I know this has been a difficult day for you," he began. "Do you feel like talking about it?"

She looked away. A tear ran down her cheek.

"May I call you Diane?"

"Yes," she replied.

"Would you feel comfortable calling me Mark?"

She turned her head back around to look at her boss. "If you like."

"Do you know why Dr. Robinson took his own life?"

Her gaze went down to the tissue she held in her hand.

"Did it have anything to do with the directive we received yesterday?"

"I don't know...it might have," she said.

"Was there anything else bothering him? Something you might know about?"

When her eyes met Mark's again, he got the feeling she wanted to tell him something. "Please," he said. "I need to know. Why don't you start by telling me what, if anything, you know of Dr. Robinson's personal life?"

"Harry was a good man," she started. "He was kind and generous. He was a bit impulsive, but he was meticulous in his work. I'd classify him as a brilliant geneticist."

"I know he had a sister. Did he speak to you of her?"

"No, we rarely shared our personal lives."

"He never spoke of his ex-wife to you?"

"Why would he do that?" She looked offended.

"Oh, no reason. I just thought he might have told you about her."

"One time he made mention of the fact that she felt neglected...wanted more of him that he was willing to offer. They never had children you know. He told me she had an affair and left him. He never elaborated. I don't think it bothered him much, if that's what you mean. I think he kind of accepted it."

"Were there any noticeable changes in his personality recently that you can remember?"

A few moments went by before she spoke again. "For some time, I began to suspect something wasn't right," she said. "Up until recently, he poured himself into his work. Then, a few weeks ago, he made some comment that I never quite understood."

"Was it about his work?"

"It was kind of like, deeper than that."

"What do you mean?"

"At first, he thought the project was going to help mankind. You know, something good...like cancer research, a cure for mental illness, autism...things like that," she paused.

"Go on," Mark encouraged her.

"Then, a few weeks ago, after we had failed in our experiment, he said the strangest thing."

"Such as?"

"He said, 'Identical locks don't necessarily have identical keys.' You know, he kind of mumbled it under his breath."

"What did you make of that?"

"I think he may have sensed some kind of flaw in his assumptions, something that made him think he was inadequate to the tasks."

"And did he elaborate?"

"I asked him what he meant, and he just waved it off, you know, kind of like it was a thought that had no real significance."

"Did you sense that as a turning point of some kind?"

"After that incident, I had the feeling he was questioning himself. You know, like our failure to create a living cell caused him to lose interest in our work."

"In what way?"

"It was little things, you know. Things that I normally wouldn't catch, but if you add them up..." she paused.

"Yes?"

"I really couldn't put my finger on it. His private discussions with Langstrum seemed to be causing more and more stress. I'm not sure anyone else noticed. I think a woman is more sensitive at picking up on male stress than men are. Look, I really need to get back to the lab..."

Mark felt he was sticking his nose into an area that made her uncomfortable and had prompted a sudden urge for her to try and end the conversation. He changed the subject.

"You said, at first he thought his research would be used for something good. What did you mean by that?"

"His brother was born with a birth defect. It was a mental handicap of some kind. I took it to mean he was retarded, something akin to that.

"He told me about it one day when we were having coffee. He said his brother died because of it. I think it was the only real emotional event that continued to haunt him. He never got over it.

"There's no doubt in my mind it's what drove him into gene research. To help others, you know. Like it was his purpose in life—to heal the sick and make up for losing his brother to a heartbreaking genetic illness. He was terribly motivated until one day." Diane paused to collect her thoughts.

"He had a conversation with Langstrum that caused him to sulk in his cubicle for over an hour. I asked him about it, but he said it was just the 'blahs' and he'd be okay. So, I left him alone for the rest of the day."

Mark decided to steer the question back to their work. "Going back to your experiment, do you think there may have been an error in the DNA sequencing?"

"Not so much an error as a miscalculation."

"Can you elaborate?"

She thought for a minute. "Okay, let me put it this way. If you add two and three, you get five, right?"

"Of course," Mark nodded.

"But what if the result is six?"

"Then obviously two, three, or both are incorrect."

"Maybe?" She looked as if she was pondering a thought.

"Do you need some time off?" Mark asked.

"No, I think I need to get my mind back on the project."

"Are you okay?"

"Yes, I'm fine, Mark."

"You *will* let me know if you'd like to talk more about the incident."

"Sure," she said in a terse sort of way.

After Diane left, Mark had the feeling there were things she didn't want to discuss with him. He wondered if she'd been involved with Robinson in some sort of personal relationship. She had appeared upset, but not overly so. Not like a lover might be with the sudden loss of their partner. If there were any guilt feelings on her part, he didn't sense it in their meeting.

* * *

Major Edward Blevins sat behind his desk at the Pentagon. He looked younger than his real age of forty-five years. His friends joked about the premature graying in his hair, and he asserted it didn't bother him — but it did. He was gaining a little bit around his belly and the women in his section kidded him about his 'cute paunch'. He said *that* didn't bother him either.

After graduating from West Point in 1944, he had served in Japan as a political officer under General Douglas MacArthur. After the Japanese occupation, he was promoted to First Lieutenant and moved into the Pentagon.

He was sorting through his mail and retrieving messages from his in-box. On the corner of his desk lay a large packet labeled *The Ladder Project*. It had been there all morning, and he was just about to open it when the phone rang.

"Blevins," he answered.

"Have you opened the Ladder packet yet?"

"Hi, Charlie, what the hell are you doing up this time of the morning?"

Lieutenant Colonel Charlie Matthews and Major Edward Blevins played handball together and even though Matthews was a grade higher in rank, they remained good friends. One year older than Blevins, during working hours, he was Edward's superior officer.

"We've got a situation," Charlie said.

"What is it?" Edward knew when it came time to dispense with the humor. When Charlie used the 'situation' word, he knew it must be serious.

"One of the geneticists on the Ladder offed himself this morning."

"Oh shit," Edward exclaimed.

"Walter's jumping through his asshole. You'd better read up on it before he calls a meeting."

"When?"

"I'm surprised he hasn't done it already."

"Roger...I'll get right on it."

Edward put down the phone, opened the packet, and read from the top page:

Dr. Harry Robinson expired near or about 0745 hours after an apparent suicide. He was discovered by his research assistant, Dr. Diane Walters, at or about 0800 hours in his apartment, located in Bldg. 786, Room 113, Barksdale AFB. Incident currently under investigation by Captain James W. Peters,

AF18513352, Strategic Air Command, Barksdale AFB, Louisiana.

The sergeant on duty knocked on the door.

"Enter," Blevins said.

"Colonel Parker wants to see you in PLC2 B-7."

Blevins gathered his material together and made his way to the meeting. The conference room was large enough for forty people, but Blevins, Walter Parker, and Charlie Matthews appeared to be the only ones in attendance.

When Blevins walked in, Charlie was pre-occupied with playing with his tie. It was a nervous tick that irritated Blevins to no end.

Charlie Matthews was blond, about Blevins' height, and a bit more handsome even though he was a year older. Matthews was highly competitive in their weekly games of handball. Too many times, he had slammed the hard rubber orb into Edward's back with such force it took his breath away.

Charlie was also single and a bit of a flirt. Charlie and Edward's wife, Sybil, would gang up on him on occasion. He never suspected the two of them had anything romantic going on—it was more like two school kids ganging up on a nerd at the nerd's expense.

Walter Parker was a striking specimen, six years older than Edward, he had not one gray strand of hair on his head. As a full-bird colonel in the U.S Marines, to him, everything was strictly by the book. During the Cuban Missile Crises, he had been present on the bow of the US destroyer, *Charles P. Cecil*, when it forced the surfacing of a Soviet submarine after it had exhausted its batteries. It had been armed with a nuclear-tipped torpedo.

A self-professed hard-ass, Walter possessed the striking characteristics of a leader. He had a wry sense of humor, almost surgical in the way he delivered his barbs.

"I have a meeting with Tom Watson and Scotty Roberts scheduled," Walter said. "They should be here in fifteen minutes. I want to settle something before they arrived."

Walter corrected his posture and stretched his neck, protruding his lower jaw. "It looks like we have trouble on the Ladder, boys." He looked at Blevins first, and then at Matthews. "Either of you have any idea as to why this..." he halted to refer to his notes, "this... Dr. Harry Robinson punched his own clock?"

Edward and Charlie shrugged.

"Have either of you spoken to Langstrum since the incident?"

"I just heard about it a few minutes before you called the meeting, Colonel," Edward said.

"I haven't spoken to Langstrum in several months," Charlie added. "I tried to get in touch with Swanson this morning, but he hasn't returned my call."

Walter scowled at the two men and cranked his squared jaw from one side of his face to the other. "Does *anyone* know what the *fuck* is going on down there?" he said, raising his voice a few decibels.

Neither man responded.

"Yesterday, we issued a directive to lock down the lab and sequester the people working on the project. Then this Robinson fellow hangs himself. Why?"

Neither Edward nor Charlie offered a reason.

"I thought we agreed when we issued this directive, *The Ladder Project* would become a high-priority issue. How could you two *bozos* let this incident go unnoticed for three goddamned hours without knowing about it?"

Charlie and Edward looked sheepishly at one another. Charlie fiddled with his tie some more.

"I want an answer on my desk *today*. I want a good reason why this Dr. Robinson offed himself, and I want it to be credible. Not some bullshit you two cooked up to placate me. If you guys can't come up with a damn good reason for this incident by 1700 hours, I'll shove the both of you into a file room so deep under this complex you won't see the light of day until it's time to collect your social security. Do I make myself clear?"

"Yessir," Edward and Charlie said in unison.

"Now, get your asses out of here and get me some answers. You've got five hours."

Blevins and Matthews excused themselves and hurried out of the room.

* * *

Mark insisted Langstrum accompany him to lunch at the private mess hall. They both ordered sandwiches and retired to the patio, where they could have some privacy.

"What happened?" Mark asked.

"I figure maybe he didn't want to live like a prisoner," Peter answered.

"I don't buy it. That answer doesn't gel with what I have been told about him. What the hell's going on, Peter?"

"What do you mean?"

"Don't play dumb with me. I've known for some time this project runs deeper than shoving DNA into *Mycoplasma mycoides.*"

Peter donned a blank stare as if he didn't know what Mark was talking about.

"Okay, let me spell it out for you. It didn't take me long to figure out what my role was going to be in this project. You've been going over my head since day one. You and Harry Swanson...God knows what that cocksucker is up to. I just read your reports and signed off on them. I've been a damned fool, Peter. I can see that now."

"Boy, when you start confessing you just don't let up, do you? Why don't you discuss these issues with Walter?"

"I've been a decoy all along, haven't I?"

"A decoy? What do you mean?"

"I've been living like a goddamned canary in a coal mine."

Peter looked puzzled.

"You guys figured if somebody was going to catch on to what was going on, they would come through me, and apparently they have. Why did Robinson hang himself?"

"I assume he didn't like the prospects of being isolated."

"That's bullshit. I've read through his performance reports. He actually thrived in this environment. What did he discover, Peter?"

"Where are you going with this, Mark?"

"Robinson's thesis was on the Cambrian explosion. Were you aware of that?"

"The sudden acceleration of life forms that occurred somewhere around 580 million years ago...sure, I was aware of it. It marked the transition from single-cell organisms to complex animals. So...what of it?"

"Something happened to the structure of DNA at that time that jumpstarted evolution, correct?"

"Well, that's the assumption, yeah, but there's really not enough evidence to come to a scientific conclusion."

"So, if someone was able to create a synthetic DNA, presumably one that would mimic one prior to the Cambrian era, and transplant it into living cells what do you suppose would be the effect?"

Langstrum did not answer.

"What do you know about *this*?" Mark produced a wrinkled graph and placed it in front of Peter.

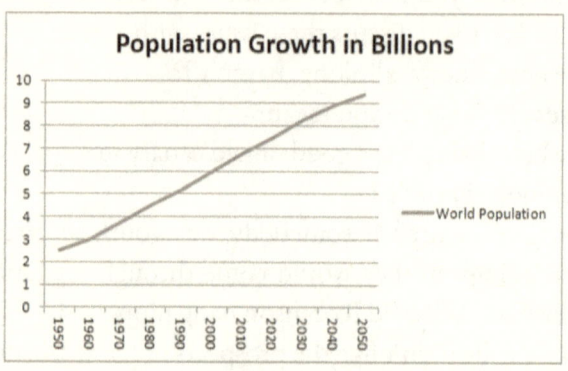

Peter picked up the paper and examined it carefully. "Where did you find this?" he said.

"Now this one," Mark laid the second graph in front of him.

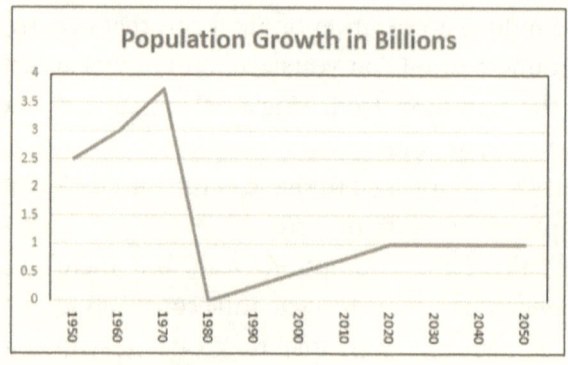

Peter's complexion turned pale.

"Could this have anything to do with Robinson's sudden decision to leave us?"

"Where did you find these?"

"I found them in the bottom of Robinson's files. I never would have seen them if they hadn't been crumpled up in the back of the drawer, after somebody took the time to remove everything else from his desk."

Mark stared at Peter, waiting for a response. "Now, Dr. Langstrum, would you like to tell me what the hell's going on?"

Peter Langstrum looked at the charts in front of him. He mumbled something to himself.

"What did you say?" Mark demanded an answer.

"Oh, it was just some crazy theory Harry came up with." He kept staring at the charts. "I thought he had given up on this nonsense." He straightened up. "I've never seen these charts before," he confessed.

"What crazy idea? What did he say?"

"It's probably nothing. It had something to do with his fascination with early Cambrian geochemical fluctuations. Harry was convinced that the Cambrian explosion was a direct result of some kind of mass extinction."

"Like an asteroid event?"

"Could have been...or it might have been a massive melt-down of methane ice...no one knows for sure." Langstrum paused. "But something happened at the onset of the Cambrian explosion that drastically altered the path of evolution, or maybe evolution didn't occur until after the event.

"Robinson saw evolution as a delicate experiment that has survived for some 530 million years."

"In other words, he felt evolution might be an anomaly?" Mark suggested.

"Yeah, that's what he thought. Life is constantly under

assault by viruses and mutations. Evolution is life's protection against extinction. Without evolution, life would have been doomed millions of years ago and Earth would be a dead planet like all of its neighbors."

"And Robinson felt that our research may threaten the path of evolution?"

"Harry believed that our research might put an end to evolution entirely. Like a child taking apart a clock and having no idea how to put it back together."

"And how would...how would we do that?"

"By purposely altering the genomic sequence of DNA, we might unintentionally switch it off. That was his theory, or maybe a better term might be *his fear*."

"Why would we do that? I thought our mission was to discover the origin of life."

"Boy, you have been out of the loop haven't you?"

Mark raised his hand up to his forehead and began rubbing it. "What in the name of God are you doing back there, Peter?"

"Well, we're attempting to create life for sure, but that's just an experiment to try and figure out how evolution really works."

"Harry thought our ultimate goal was to attempt to redirect evolution?" Mark said.

"No. As I said, Harry thought the mission was to try and put an end to evolution."

Mark stared at Peter for a moment before he said anything else. "That's insane...isn't it?"

* * *

When Mark arrived back at his desk, there was a message waiting for him. He picked up the phone and dialed the Pentagon.

"Speak," Walter said.

"You asked me to call?"

"What the hell's going on down there, Mark?"

"We're trying to find out."

"Well, was this Robinson fellow nuts or what?"

"I don't know, Walter." He wanted to tell him about his meeting with Langstrum, but he thought better of it. After all, it was just a crazy theory offered by Peter, and it might not have anything to do with Dr. Robinson's suicide. It might not have anything to do with anything, for that matter.

"Mark, I'm losing my patience here. If you and Peter can't come to a plausible conclusion, I'll send somebody down there who will." He hung up in Mark's ear.

Just then, Mark's intercom buzzed. Mark pushed the 'answer' switch and spoke to the sergeant on duty.

"What's up?" Mark said.

"There's a Major Blevins from the Pentagon on the line. He wants to talk to you."

"Go ahead and patch him through."

"Mark, how are you doing?" Blevins said.

"Hi, Edward. Not too good at the moment."

"Are you with Peter?"

"Not now, we just got back from lunch."

"Have you guys come up with anything new?"

"About Robinson's suicide? We don't have a clue."

"Did you talk to his co-workers?"

"He worked with Diane Walters. They were pretty much isolated from the other teams. She said something was bothering him, but she couldn't put her finger on it."

"Anything else?"

"Peter tells me he'd been upset about some radical idea concerning the possible derailment of evolution."

"Hmmm..." Blevins grunted. "And?"

"He was obsessed with the Cambrian explosion. I found some disturbing population growth charts in his desk after somebody had cleaned it out. We don't know who. It had to be someone in the office though, because no one else had access to it."

"What kind of charts?"

"Well, it looks like the first one was a projection of future world-wide population growth, and the second one looked like some kind of uh...alteration of the first one."

"Do you think it was his assistant who rifled his desk?"

"Could be...I was going to have another chat with her when you called."

"Call me after you talk to her. Look, Mark, Walter has given us 'til 1700 hours to come up with something or all hell's going to break loose around here. Shit rolls downhill. Do you get my drift?"

"Yeah, I'm already standing in it up to my neck. I'll call as soon as I have something new to report."

Mark hung up the phone and went back to Peter's office.

"We need to talk to Diane."

Mark found Diane hunched over her desk, going through a printout of tables.

"Diane, I apologize for interrupting you again, but we have a situation here and the Pentagon wants us to clear it up. We've got three hours to come up with an acceptable reason for Harry's actions."

"I've already told you what I know," she said.

Mark pulled the charts out of his coat pocket and showed them to her.

"Have you seen these charts before?"

"Yes," she said.

"The second one, what do you make of it?"

"It's just a theory Harry had. It doesn't mean anything."

"Who cleaned out Harry's desk this morning? Was it you?"

"No, I never went in his desk...ever."

"Do you know who might have?"

"Swanson...I think it was Swanson."

"Come with me. Peter and I need to talk with you."

On the way to the conference room, Mark stopped at the sergeant's desk.

"Where's Harry Swanson?"

"He hasn't come back from lunch."

"Let me know the minute he arrives."

"Will do," the sergeant responded.

Mark and Diane joined Langstrum who was already in the conference room waiting for them.

"Hi, Diane, you okay?" Peter said.

She shrugged. "Okay, I guess."

Mark pulled a chair out and Diane sat down. Then he seated himself. He put the second chart on the table.

"Now, tell us what you know about this," he demanded.

Diane looked at Peter. "It's okay," Peter said. "Tell Mark what he wants to know."

"Harry thought the Pentagon wanted us to figure out how to alter DNA so they could shut down evolution," she said.

"But it would take generations before it would have any effect, wouldn't it?" Mark asked. "What would be the purpose?"

"To engineer the perfect race."

"That still doesn't explain this chart," Mark exclaimed, jamming his finger on the point that was labeled '1980' in the second chart.

Diane and Peter exchanged glances. Mark directed his attention to Peter.

"Harry had this crazy notion the Pentagon planned a mass, global extinction," Peter said.

"Extinction of what?" Mark looked perplexed.

"Us," Peter replied.

"You mean us, as in everybody...the entire goddamn planet?"

"I didn't say I believed him."

"But why? For what reason?"

"I believe Hitler called it, 'sterilization of the undesirables.' But in this case, it would result in a docile race, lacking the genes of their warring ancestors."

Mark's mouth dropped open.

"Well, it's not an entirely bad idea when you think about it," Peter said.

"What do you mean?" Mark choked. "The murder of three and a quarter billion human beings is not such a *bad idea*?"

"I'm not advocating it...God no. I'm just saying it *would* solve a lot of problems."

"You can't be serious," Mark stuttered.

"Well, when you think about it, how are we going to feed ten-billion people in the year 2050? How about energy, clean water, disease, wars? The addition of every new, human being ups the odds of mass extinction. The white race is already on the fast track to extermination. Some well-meaning, bureaucrat might decide intervention is better than chance."

"And...you think Harry Robinson was convinced of this?" He looked at Diane.

"Yeah, I think he was," she answered.

"Holy shit," Mark exclaimed. "Well, he *was* a goddamned nut case." Mark thought for a minute. "There's our answer. He was some fruitcake that had convinced himself he was being forced down a path with the ultimate goal of destroying humanity."

"What if he was right?"

"What do you mean? No normal, human being would think it was right to eliminate the *entire* human race."

"No, and neither did Harry," Peter said. "But let's just assume for the time being that he *was* right. Maybe that's the plan the Pentagon has for saving the planet. Are you going to be the one that tells them we know about it?"

"Well, this is pre...pre...preposterous," Mark scoffed.

"Preposterous?" Diane said. "A lot of people thought the Manhattan Project was preposterous, didn't they? And that was only to shorten one war that was already over. Just how far might our own government go to 'save the world'?"

"Mark," Peter said looking at his watch, "you've got two and a half hours to decide on whether you're going to tell Walter and that bunch of politicians in Washington why Harry *really* killed himself."

Chapter Three
2018

A nna May Lee was twenty-years of age. Her real parents died in a plane crash a few months after she was born and she was raised by her maternal grandmother. Through her formative years, she had been an exceptionally bright child. Early on, she was enrolled in a class of gifted students, graduated from high school at the age of fifteen, and immediately entered the California Institute of Technology. After she acquired her master's degree in molecular biology, she was currently working on her PhD defense.

Unlike her grandmother and her mother before her, Anna May was tall and slender with features more akin to the young ladies on the cover of a New York fashion magazine——somewhat of a handicap for a woman in the business of molecular biology.

When she spoke, even in a full-length lab coat, men found it difficult to pay attention to her lecture. It never made her self-conscious, but it threatened her professional facade. Consequently, while giving her presentations she tended to use a lot of computer-generated slides and graphics — hiding in the shadows whenever possible.

Anna May sat crossed legged in the sand at Waimanalo Beach Park in Hawaii with a computer on her lap. She had a good view of Rabbit Island off the eastern coast of Oahu; but she wasn't looking at the rabbit—she was concentrating on her keystrokes. The blue-green, waves gently caressed the shore as she worked on her dissertation. She estimated another three days on her thesis, and she would be finished.

A red, Mercedes convertible entered the park from Kalanianaole Highway and parked under a grove of Banyan trees. Wearing a tank-top and cut off's, Bob Cook approached her, bent down, and brushed a light kiss across her cheek. He set an ice cold, Gatorade G4 in the sand next to her. Bob and Anna May were celebrating the 1st anniversary of their meeting at that very spot.

At twenty-five, Bob was a lean, tall and muscular fellow. He was taking his annual vacation from his desk job with the FBI and had occupied the majority of his time-off watching Anna May work. Being careful not to interfere with her train of thought, he gathered up his surfboard and waded out into the Pacific Ocean.

The surf was calm with a gentle shore break, hardly a scene for catching a tube ride, but this was a working vacation for Anna May, and Bob was content to paddle around and peer at tiny sea creatures while she typed. Off in the distance, an enormous aircraft carrier sailing out of Pearl Harbor seemed to slip silently over the edge of the world.

A message appeared on Anna May's computer screen and immediately caught her attention. *"North Korean researcher, Kim Bong Hwa, rumored to have made a significant break-*

through in evolution research." The message came from a tweet she had been following with some interests.

During the past year, the North Koreans appeared to deviate from their quest for a nuclear weapon and moved into the field of molecular biology. As far back as 2004, it had been reported that North Korean prisoners were forced to act as guinea pigs in the quest for bio-chemical weapons. Kwan-li-so No. 22 Haengyong Prison housed an estimated 50,000 men, women, and children. Reports of medical experiments conducted on detainees were growing more and more disturbing.

The new field of Synthetic Biology made possible by developments in genome sequencing and genetic engineering created a novel approach for the creation of augmented pathogens. It was no secret that the North Koreans were developing biological weapons and she supposed they were probably obtaining complete pathogen genomes from unscrupulous DNA providers. The National Science Advisory Board for Biosecurity seemed impotent in enforcing its 'Code of Conduct'.

The US Department of Health and Human Services had addressed the issue by publishing 'Screening Framework Guidance for Synthetic Double-Stranded DNA Providers' with the expected results—the honest providers tended to comply, while the dishonest providers tended to ignore the regulations entirely. There was no doubt—North Korea would have no trouble getting whatever it wanted.

This recent announcement regarding a 'breakthrough in evolution', coupled with a familiar name, caused Anna May to ponder over her grandmother's diaries, locked in a trunk back at her apartment in Pasadena. She made a mental note to reread the material as soon as the couple returned to California.

Her maternal grandmother had introduced her to molecular biology when she was just old enough to read. She had gained the young girl's interest simply by convincing her there were deep-dark secrets that only she could read about, and she made her promise never to reveal what she had read to another living soul. The curiosity factor was just enough to lessen the amount of time Anna May spent in front of the television. By the third grade, while her classmates struggled over addition, subtraction, and multiplication tables, Anna May was solving mathematical equations out of college algebra books. It wasn't long after that she began reading 'College Physics' by Raymond Serway and Chris Vuille.

That night, over dinner at one of her favorite restaurants —*Beijing,* in the *Royal Hawaiian Shopping Center*—she was enjoying a serving of minced chicken and sweet corn soup from the *A dinner,* when Bob said, "You been awfully quiet since we got back to the hotel...problems with your thesis?"

"No," she replied. "I'm almost done."

"Well, what is it? You seem preoccupied."

"Do you remember me telling you about my Gran Diane?"

"You mean the mysterious grandmother that was working on a top-secret experiment for the government in the late sixties?"

"When we get home, I want you to read some of the material she left in her trunk."

"You mean about gene research?" he laughed. "My education is in criminology. Biology was my worst subject, remember?"

"I'm not so sure there wasn't a crime involved in what she was doing."

"Sweet, old, gray-headed Gran Diane, involved in a crime? Surely you jest."

"No, silly...I don't think *she* was doing anything illegal. She was employed by the US government." She paused. "What do you know about the North Koreans?"

"They're assholes," Bob laughed.

"That's an intelligent, scientific evaluation if I ever heard one," she chuckled.

"I told you, I was horrible at science," he admitted.

"I got a tweet today that made me recall something I read in her diaries."

"Really?"

"Her research assistant committed suicide at about the same time the project ended."

"When he lost his job?"

"No... He had this crazy idea the government was planning a mass extinction of the human race."

"I can't buy that," Bob scoffed.

"Neither did Gran. But wait, there's more. He believed their research involved putting an end to evolution as a prelude to creating a perfect race that would repopulate the world."

"After killing off the seven-billion residents that lived here?" Bob said.

"Back then it would have been more like four billion...but yeah, I think he did."

"The guy was obviously a nut-case."

Anna May began pondering a thought. "Up until this year, the North Koreans were furiously trying to develop nuclear weapons."

"Uh huh."

"Why did they suddenly stop?"

"Threats, sanctions... who knows? Maybe it was over their pay grade."

"I thought you Feds were supposed to be up on this stuff."

"Ask me anything you want about breaking into computers

and I'm your man. But I know less about biology than I know about world politics," he said.

"Perhaps," she said. "But I don't think threats and sanctions had anything to do with it. I think they shifted their interests elsewhere for another reason.

"Did you ever hear of a Korean by the name of Kim Bong Hwa?"

"You mean like...Kim Jong-il?"

"A nephew, I think."

"No, that name doesn't ring a bell."

"Kim Bong Hwa studied molecular biology at Caltech. Then he returned to North Korea to work for his famous uncle. If I'm not mistaken, his thesis had something to do with 'interrupting evolution'. When I got the tweet today, he immediately popped in my mind.

"Many environmentalists," she continued, "believe the perfect population for the Earth is no more than one-half billion people. We now have fourteen times that many and they believe an extinction-level event, such as an asteroid slamming into Mother Earth, would be a *good* thing."

"So Earth becomes a dead planet like Mars, and everybody's happy?"

"Yes, I think there are some out there that would see that as an improvement."

"But man wouldn't exist anymore, so who would be here to enjoy the solitude?"

"Doesn't matter...it would be good for the *Earth*."

"That's dumb," Bob said.

"Put yourself in God's shoes for a second. You look down and what do you see? The world is out of control. Wars, famine, disease...we are creating our own living Hell right here on Earth. It has to end badly.

"If a group of brilliant, politically motivated geneticists could figure out a way to kill off the rest of us, they could take control of a *new* Earth and create a perfect world for their descendants; and to ensure nothing like this would ever happen again, they would simply turn off evolution and create their own species modeled after themselves."

"The God complex on steroids...is turning off evolution even a possibility?"

"Sure, it's already been done."

"Really?"

"Each living cell has a mechanism biologists refer to as 'mutation machinery'. When a living cell is damaged beyond repair, this mechanism kicks in to open the floodgates of evolution, allowing it to survive, although a bit altered.

"For example, by subjecting E. coli to compounds that block a protein called LexA we can shut off the bacteria's mutation machinery and prevent the evolution of the pathogen's resistance to antibiotics. Theoretically, there's no reason why we can't do that with every living cell.

"Floyd Romesberg from the Scripps Research Institute has proven evolution is subject to intervention and not an unstoppable force by any means."

"Whoa," Bob said. "Sugar, you're getting way over my pay grade here. So, evolution is a product of cellular damage?"

"Right, and without cellular damage, nothing changes."

"Why?"

"Because the body has to survive. So rather than give up and die, it simply changes into something else —— at the cellular level that is."

"So, let me get this straight. If a government could wipe out its population and replace it with subjects designed to be peaceful and obedient, and they were able to keep them that way without using force...that would be a communist dictator's dream," he said. "Do you think that's what your grandmother was working on?"

"Not knowingly, but I think her research assistant got the idea that was exactly what was going on, and that's why he ended his own life."

"And you think that may be what the North Koreans have planned for us?"

"Well, like you said, it would be a communist dictator's dream, right?"

Bob gave her a funny look. "If it were anyone but you saying it, I'd think you required psychiatric help."

"Well?" she said.

Back in the room, Bob interrupted Anna May. "You know, I've been thinking about what you said earlier and I just thought of something. There's a fringe group out there that believes our government is stacking the deck of evolution by aiding weaker members of society."

Anna May looked up from her computer screen. "I never really thought about it, but yes, there is an argument for politically assisted evolution. I'm not so sure it's valid, but I can see how some people might look at it that way."

"One-thousand years ago, only the strong survived to procreate," he went on. "The slow and the weak were eaten by wild animals or succumbed to disease. Technology has stepped in to change the game. The 'slow' drive cars and fly on jet planes," he went on. "The 'weak' get free health-care, vitamins and medicine. Health-care is rationed, and the government decides who gets it and how much of it they get.

"There is some reasoning for letting the old die without treatment, although immoral to be sure, but to deny food and medical care to people who differ politically is right out of

Hitler, Stalin and Mao. If we woke up one morning and found that all technology was rationed according to one political majority over another, what would be the effect on world population?"

Anna May took her hands off the keyboard. "Bob, I love you dearly, sweetheart. But I really need to finish this section. Could you just be quiet for a little while longer, and then we can talk about it?"

Bob let out a disapproving grunt and retired to the corner to sulk over a John Grisham mystery he purchased at the gift shop. "She's done it to me again," he muttered. "She gets me interested in one subject, and then she tells me she's too busy to talk about it."

"Bob!" she scolded.

* * *

Bob Cook moved to California when his father took a job as a civil servant working for the US Justice Department. He attended Loyola High School, played on the tennis team, and graduated as valedictorian of his class. He went on to earn his masters at CSU Los Angeles where he majored in computer science. He got a job with the Federal Bureau of Investigation one year before he met Anna May Lee. He had a six-month affair with a law student that ended in complete disaster. The experience had been so bad he refused to date for six months after they split up.

He boarded the plane at LAX with just enough clothes and personal items to last for one day, and upon arrival in Hawaii he went directly to the Ala Moana shopping center in Honolulu to buy clothes and supplies. Then he crashed at his rented studio apartment at the Aston on Waikiki.

Bob was four years older than Anna May but emotionally her inferior. He felt an animal attraction for her the first time he saw her lying on the beach in Hawaii the year before. At first, he wondered why a beautiful woman like Anna May would be alone on the beach. He waited for a respectable time fully expecting a boyfriend or husband to show up at any moment. Finally, he worked up the nerve to walk over and introduce himself — but first, he took off his watch and shoved it in his pocket.

"Excuse me," he said. "Do you know what time it is?"

Anna May took one look at him and immediately noticed the pale, white band around his wrist where his watch had been present only seconds before.

"Are you trying to pick me up?" she asked.

Bob saw she was staring at the obvious mark on his wrist. Rolling his wrist, he sheepishly replied, "I'm not much good at this. Please forgive me," then he turned to walk away.

"You didn't answer my question." She laughed.

Bob stopped dead in his tracks, turned and said, "Obviously, I was just making a complete idiot of myself."

"What's your name?" she insisted.

"Robert C. Cook at your service."

"What do you do?" She said it like she didn't expect an interesting answer.

"I work for the FBI."

"A 'G' Man," she started. "Here in Honolulu?"

"No, in California."

"In LA?" she asked.

"Yeah, I work in an office downtown."

"I live in Pasadena myself."

"Really?" he smiled.

"What do you do with the FBI?"

"I'm an IT specialist for the government ...and you?"

"PhD student at Caltech."

"What field?"

"Molecular biology," she said.

That's the way it started. They had dinner that night and the night after, and every night for the duration of their time in Hawaii. It was Bob's first time dating an intelligent woman. He had always managed to find girls whose major accomplishment was turning oxygen into carbon dioxide. Anna May was the complete opposite. He marveled at her superior intelligence. On their first date, he imagined she would find him boring, but she found his personality irresistible. He made her laugh.

Two weeks after they returned from their vacations, they rented a neat, three-bedroom California Craftsman home on Arden Road in Pasadena.

Anna May closed her lap-top and changed into her night-gown. She found Bob lying in the bed and staring at the ceiling. She snuggled up close and said, "You mad at me?"

"No, honey, I'm not mad...just thinking."

"What are you thinking about?"

"My father used to say there was an intentional 'dumbing down' of America."

"Where on earth did he get that idea?" she said.

"He grew up in the South during the civil rights era."

"Well, that might have something to do with it. Do you believe he was right?"

"No, but you know the United States is ranked eighteenth in education behind Belgium, Poland, the Czech Republic and South Korea, and getting further behind every year," he said. "I can see why he thought it might have been intentional.

"Parents of American kids can't choose the schools their kids go to. That's the difference. They're a lot of shitty schools out there. We were both lucky to have the resources to get into private ones.

"So, money affects the evolutionary process. Rich kids mate with rich kids and create more rich kids. Poor kids mate with poor kids and create more poor kids."

"I suppose, but being poor doesn't make them bad," Anna May interjected.

"No, but it helps, doesn't it?" he said.

Bob was being herded down a country road—one of billions heading nowhere. Both sides of the trail were lined with fields of cane. As he looked into the cane, he saw young men and women of the Korean People's Army dressed in brown uniforms with brown caps and peering out at him. The faces dissolved back into the canes as far as he could see.

The men were thin, lean, almost emaciated. Their slanted eyes were sunk deep into their eye sockets. The women were small and flat-chested. Except for the fairness of their skin, they were undistinguishable from the males. Each one held a rifle. None were smiling. They had a look of utter hatred in their eyes. They were firing their weapons at him. The bullets whizzed by his body —each one within a centimeter of striking him. He could feel the heat from each slug as they burned his skin. The bullets made no sound.

Bob awoke from his dream. He was sweating profusely, as if he had been running a marathon. His heart was racing, and adrenalin coursed through his body.

* * *

Chung-hee Kyung was born in a North Korean prison. His parents were prisoners in Camp Number Thirteen, isolated in the mountains north of the North Korean capital of Pyongyang. As a reward for good behavior, they were selected at random and put together in a cell for five days. Nine months later, Chung-hee Kyung was expelled onto a dirt floor. His earliest memories were his constant hunger for food.

The little boy lived with his mother who worked every day from five in the morning and would return around midnight. She oftentimes beat him. He learned nothing about common humanity. He developed no feelings for love, compassion, or forgiveness. His mom had made mistakes, so it was only natural for him to live like that. He never thought to question why.

Chung-hee Kyung was a victim of the "hereditary rule". When an individual committed certain crimes as defined by the North Korean government, he or she and their entire immediate family were imprisoned. Three generations of torture and punishment followed to 'weed out the bad seed'—a common practice in North Korean society. Why he was allowed to be born remained a mystery to him. Better to suffocate in the after-birth on the filthy floor of his mother's cell. God did not exist in the Democratic People's Republic of North Korea. There was no entity to plead to for help.

During his pre-adolescent years, he was forced to lie on his back with a pole jammed in behind his knees as other children were instructed to trample on his legs. His fingernails remained split and broken because guards inserted sharp bamboo under them.

He attended school in the mornings, where he was taught to read and write. His instructors were guards who wore pistols and carried sticks to beat the children. Once, he witnessed the beating to death of a little girl in his class. No one came to claim the body. She was discarded in a ditch that ran around the perimeter of the complex.

In the afternoons, he was sent to the mountains to do hard labor. There he could catch mice, rats, snakes and worms for his eternally hungry stomach.

Friendships and closeness did not exist. Everyone knew they had to fend for themselves. Anyone could be an informer. The society was structured in such a way that mothers informed on sons, and sons informed on fathers. Depending on the 'crimes', the reprisals varied in their intensity.

When the day came for Chung-hee Kyung to attend secondary school, he was separated from his mother and placed in a dormitory. There was no education provided. From the age of twelve, there was nothing but work—but they called it *secondary school*.

At the age of fourteen, he was allowed to see his mother and an unknown brother. Then he was suddenly dragged out of the dormitory by guards, thrown into a cell and subjected to unspeakable torture.

The guards chopped off a finger with a crude knife, beat him senseless, stripped him naked and held him over a fire supported by ropes tethered to his feet and arms, with a hook through his belly to lift him up when it became apparent that he would lose consciousness. His mother and brother had attempted to escape, and the purpose of his treatment was to find out if he knew anything about their actions. But he knew nothing and couldn't tell them anything. The torture lasted for seven months.

He was taken to another section of the camp where he expected to be executed. He was led into a compound where his mother and brother were tied to posts. His brother was shot dead, and his mother was strangled to death. Just before she died, she looked directly at him. He avoided her gaze.

From that day forward, a miserable life was transformed to that of daily, naked horrors. He was taken to a prison where he was beaten daily. The other children—hungry, filthy little animals like himself—stole his food and threw rocks at him. He despised his mother and brother for what they had done. Years went by with no respite.

One day he found himself with another prisoner in an open field located in a 'specialized controlled zone'. The guards were nowhere in sight, and the 3,300-volt electric fence was only a few meters away. Their hunger fueled their obsession to escape. If they didn't run then, they may never get another chance.

His co-worker bolted first and threw himself against the fence. There were sparks and the smell of burning flesh. The boy had been electrocuted. Chung-hee Kyung crawled out over the smoking body and made his way down a narrow path and hid behind some rocks.

He expected the guards to come looking for him, but no one did. Catching a snake, he ripped at its flesh with his teeth until he managed to consume all of it. He felt remorse for leaving the other boy behind, but he didn't quite understand the feeling. In a short time, he felt nothing at all and went his own way. Somehow, he managed to make his way across the border and into China. Along the way, he managed to stay out of sight. From there he made it to Hong Kong, where he obtained a visa from the South Korean embassy and ended up in Seoul.

North Korea is a prison occupied by twenty-two million inmates, with ten percent being held in concentration camps. Forced abortions and mass murder was not enough to control the exploding population. New and improved methods were needed to solve the problem.

Kim Il-sung's interest in DNA research began in the early sixties as camps were established in Jungpyung, a South Hamkyung province, for the purpose of housing people of small statue to prevent dwarves from multiplying.

Now, Chung Hee Kyung sat patiently in a South Korean restaurant waiting for an appointment with *the American*.

Chapter Four
The Discovery

When Bob and Anna May arrived at Honolulu International Airport, they checked their luggage and went through security. Anna May fed her ID card through a reader and placed her right-hand over a fingerprint scanner. Her picture immediately appeared on a computer screen located in front of an agent. The officer examined it, confirmed her identity, and waved her through. The entire process took less than ten seconds. Bob followed along behind her.

During the flight, Anna May went to the Internet and surfed the web for information about North Korea. She googled 'Kim Bong Hwa' and found several references, one pointing to a villa on a reservoir in the Samsuk District of Pyongyang, one of seventeen belonging to Kim Jong-un. There was also a mountain by the same name in South Korea, but no mention of Kim Bong Hwa the molecular biologist anywhere—not even in the Caltech alumni list, and no mention in the molecular biology department's list of researchers.

Strange, she thought. The tweet she received while in Honolulu had come with no reference to the original tweeter's name. Only the presence of the retweet icon told her it had originated from an unknown source.

Pulling up Kim Jong-il's family tree at Wikipedia showed no reference to the mysterious nephew. She glanced through the excerpt from a book authored by the left-leaning journalist, Bruce Cumings, a professor of history at the University of Chicago where he stated North Korea was the 'eternal enemy' of the United States and wrote, 'American planes dropped tens of thousands of bombs and many tons of napalm on cities in North Korea during the Korean War' which began in 1950. Consequently, he claimed North Korea was a country with at least 15,000 underground facilities. There was little doubt in Anna May's mind—Kim Bong Hwa was in one of them.

The Internet was teaming with information about North Korea's nuclear ambitions, but not one, single google search of 'North Korea', 'research' and the words 'DNA', 'Molecular Biology', or 'genetics' produced any useful data. It appeared as if North Korea had no interest in molecular biology research whatsoever.

Why did Kim Bong Hwa study for his PhD in Molecular Biology anyway? she wondered. *Those damn North Koreans are up to something, and it's not nuclear in nature.*

* * *

Bob and Anna May arrived in Los Angeles at 7:30 p.m., made their way through the terminal and collected their luggage. It was a beautiful sunset in Los Angeles, and they managed to catch a glimpse of it right before the sun dropped off the edge of the Pacific Ocean. Bob had opted to not drive his GMC Tahoe to the terminal, and leave it in long-term parking, so they caught a cab outside of the baggage claim area.

Since the Border Patrol had been disbanded earlier in the year, and been replaced by individual state's National Guard units, a person was asking for trouble by leaving their car parked in a parking lot anywhere in Southern California. Unattended cars had a way of finding their way across the border and into Mexico before the owner could drop his keys into his pocket.

While in Hawaii, one of the things they missed the most was a place to find good, Italian food. They had the driver drop them off at Gale's Restaurant & Bar on South Fair Oaks Avenue. The restaurant closed at 9:00 p.m. on weekdays and they were the last couple to be allowed in for dinner.

Gale's had a quaint atmosphere with brick, interior walls displaying modern, Italian art. With its casual table settings and open kitchen, separated from the dining room by a marble-clad counter, Gale's suggested Mediterranean rusticity, but with a few elegant touches. Waiters wore slacks with white dress shirts rolled slightly above the wrist.

Anna May ordered Zuppe di Pesce, a dish made primarily of crayfish, mussels, razor clams and red mullet. Bob ordered his usual, Country Style Tuscan Steak with fresh asparagus and chopped tomatoes. Anna May settled on a half-bottle of Frank Family from Napa Valley and Bob ordered Ferrari-Carano Sienna decanted in Sonoma County.

The dinner was delicious. They didn't talk much throughout the meal. Anna May was anxious to open Diane's trunk when she arrived at home and Bob wasn't much of a conversationalist while he was eating.

The couple arrived home at 11 PM, which was only 8 PM in Honolulu, so neither Bob nor Anna May felt much like turning in. Anna May began going through Diane's trunk, sorting out her notes and categorizing them.

"Have you read all this?" Bob asked.

"Most of it, but it's been a while. A lot of it I didn't quite understand at the time. I've been meaning to go back through it, but I always had something else to do."

Bob poured a glass of wine.

"We need to take this all to the den and spread it out," he said. "Else, we'll never be able to make heads nor tails of it."

The trunk was heavy and had been stored in the bottom of a walk-in closet. It took Bob and Anna May pulling together to drag it out. They began taking piles of papers out of the trunk and setting them on the floor of the den.

"How should we do this?" he asked.

"The first thing we need to do is to separate the personal stuff from what looks like research material. Then we'll re-sort each pile in chronological order."

"There's not enough light in here," Bob said as he pulled a lamp out of the corner of the room and positioned it in the center. Walking over to a walnut table Diane bought in an upscale furniture store on Rodeo Drive, he switched on the XM Satellite radio, permanently set to the "Real Jazz" channel. Les Davis, the host, was introducing Sergio Salvatore's recording, *Which Way Did She Go?* from the album entitled *Dark Sand*. Bob and Anna May were both huge fans of Sergio Salvatore since they discovered they had both attended his concert with Christos Rafalides when they had appeared many years before at Birdland.

By 1:00 a.m. Anna May began to get tired. "There's some material here that doesn't look familiar. Gran must have added it before she died," she said.

Finally, they both headed for the bedroom. Bob was asleep before his head hit the pillow—Anna May was close behind.

She had one more day left on her vacation, so the next morning, after Bob left for work, she started reading.

For the first year, the research appeared to be more-or-less straight-forward. The emphasis seemed to concentrate on the creation of life. In the first months of the second year, Diane had made some references to the teams diverging along different paths. Although each team was forbidden to discuss their research with the other teams, Diane's notes indicated one-half of the team appeared to stop working on artificial life and began concentrating on the process of evolution—a topic not mentioned when the project began.

Toward the end of the second year, Diane made references to a marked change in Harry Robinson's character. She became concerned that he was 'losing his focus'. Then, Anna May began to read the new material she had not seen before.

Three months before the project ended, her grandmother made reference to some of Harry Robinson's arguments with Langstrum. He had found out about the other team's research on evolution, and he had warned Peter that altering the normal course of evolution was a 'dangerous idea'.

Robinson's concern seemed to center around his belief that if cells were not allowed to evolve, they would lose their ability to mutate and become resistant to newer antibiotics. Peter argued, human evolution had remained static for the past 40,000 years and if they could prevent the evolution of new bacteria that threatened human existence, the creation of new drugs would no longer be necessary. Harry countered that new bacteria could arrive from "out of nowhere", maybe encased in meteorites that crashed through the atmosphere by the hundreds of thousands every day, or from an as of yet undiscovered bug lying dormant somewhere in Africa or South America.

Harry had extrapolated the argument to what he believed was the obvious intention of the project—to replace all human life on earth with a new race of humans that would be more to the liking of the government.

Anna May searched through the documents, carefully looking for anything that would corroborate Robinson's fears, but she found nothing. A chill ran through her. If the North Koreans had somehow gained access to *The Ladder Project*, and Robinson's suspicions were true, the crazy bastards had access to twenty-two million human beings to test the hypothesis. Could that be the reason why they continued to abduct the Japanese?

* * *

Chung-hee Kyung sat in a handmade chair in a dark corner of the Design Café, located in the center of Seoul, South Korea. He was sipping a lukewarm cup of hot chocolate as Michael Hager walked over, accompanied by a short Korean man wearing dark sunglasses and a beard. Chung-hee Kyung assumed it was Hager's interpreter.

Colonel Hager was a big man, about thirty-five years of age, six feet tall, clean shaven, with short hair—he looked like a typical officer in the U.S Marines. Dressed in civilian attire, he wore brown slacks with a green shirt opened at the collar and a brown sports coat—no tie.

The two men sat down facing Chung-hee Kyung. Hager's companion introduced himself as simply, 'Dong-sun'. Chung-hee Kyung spoke no English and had trouble with the South Korean's accent, so Dong-sun carried on the conversation in *Cháoxiǎnyǔ*, the traditional North Korean language. The younger North Korean appeared impressed that Dong-sun spoke his native language so well.

Chung-hee told Dong-sun about his thirty-five-month

journey through China and Southeast Asia to reach South Korea, and how he was almost arrested on several occasions and would have been returned to the North Korean labor camps. In which case he would have been summarily tortured and executed.

Hager listened intently as Dong-sun translated his comments and he treated Chung-hee Kyung with respect, something Chung-hee Kyung never expected from anyone, especially an American.

Chung-hee Kyung had always been led to believe that South Korea was an American colony and a springboard for a future invasion into the DPRK. It was going to be difficult for Hager to gain his trust.

There had been talk of unifying the two countries, but South Koreans were split on the possibility of unification with the North, citing economic concerns as their primary worry. Chung-hee Kyung related that it had been difficult for him to 'fit in'.

His recounting of treatment in the North Korean prisons rang typical of the many experiences that had been echoed by other refugees that had escaped but hearing about it filled Hager with rage.

The North Korean Human Rights Act of 2008 had expired in 2012, and a veil of secrecy made it increasingly difficult to get accurate information as to the fate of the North Korean population.

Dong-sun showed little emotion to Chung-hee's story. He had heard it all before. Dong-sun told the boy that they wanted to keep an open-line of communications as they might have a 'small' job for him in the future. He offered Chung-hee Kyunga a stipend of 1.5 million South Korean Won per-month, equivalent to about $1,200 US if he would continue to meet with them. Chung-hee was shocked, but he accepted the offer graciously and without question.

* * *

Kim Bong Hwa sat crouched over a black countertop scarred by acid and other chemicals. His laboratory in North Korea was an intimidating place with cold linoleum floors and glaring bright fluorescent lights.

Earlier, he had participated in the willful murder of fifty North Korean women who were forced to eat poisoned cabbage leaves under the fear of reprisals against their families. He filmed the entire event so he could make copious notes about the killings and the butchering of the bodies that occurred after-wards...all in the interest of scientific study.

At Kwan-li-so No.22, Haengyong, he had overseen labora-tories equipped for poison gas, suffocation gas and blood experi-ments. By and by, he had grown bored with the senseless killings and became extremely excited when he received the packet enti-tled, *The Ladder Project.*

Kim Bong Hwa had spent two years examining *The Ladder Project,* and with his team of one-hundred molecular biology subordinates, he was well on his way to solving the problem of creating synthetic life.

His handicap was dealing with the inferior education of his associates. Progress was slowed by the necessity of assisting all one hundred of them in their experiments, but he made-up for it by using humans as guinea pigs in his trial-and error exercises. He was fortunate to have an endless supply of test subjects from the 50,000 candidates interned in the prison. If he ran out there, there were several million more available from other prisons.

His new project was in the study and creation of transgenic

humans through the deliberate modifications of the human genome to affect inherited characteristics.

Within the nucleus of cells found in every animal, there are genes made up of DNA which can be altered by introducing additional genes at the embryonic stage. It accomplishes its task by 'knocking-out' the functioning of a targeted gene thus affecting the way an individual develops and behaves. The result is a slightly modified version of what the organism would have become had it developed into a living, breathing human being normally. Unfortunately, his test subjects didn't live long enough to prove that to be a fact.

In his estimation, aggression, hope, disobedience, and the desire for independence were the four greatest threats to the North Korean way of life. By removing these traits, he and his superiors would create a utopian society—ruled by a communistic tyranny, of course.

In his latest work, female prisoners were forced to mate with male inmates and then experiments were done on the living fetuses throughout the term of their pregnancies. Sometimes the fetuses would be aborted, dissected, and the materials collected were used to affect the fetuses of later impregnated women.

A breakthrough in Kim Bong Hwa's research had resulted in the speeding up of the growth process so the gestation period was reduced to only one month. The deformities were simply not a factor to be considered. It was the genes he was interested in. By the time a child reached nine weeks of age, he could be tested to determine if progress had been made in removing the undesired traits.

There were several bothersome side effects, which usually resulted in the death of the host before the fetus was sufficiently developed to live outside the womb — the main one being the splitting of the host's skin and muscle tissue during the accelerated gestation process, causing undue stress on the fetus.

He solved this problem by cutting the outer skin and muscles of the female subjects and controlling the pain with various drugs until the fetus had developed to the point where it could be removed through a caesarean procedure. Then the hosts were merely discarded.

Using his access to the Internet, he was able to gather the details of hundreds of experiments that had been done on lab rats, chimpanzees, and rabbits. He would then try each one on his human subjects, always with horrifying results.

In other experiments, he injected DNA segments into the embryos of women during the ovulation phase. After impregnation was a success, he extracted the resulting fertilized eggs and performed experiments on them.

To date, he had tortured and murdered a total of 1,512 prisoners—the number of murdered fetuses remained a mystery. He felt certain that his aim of creating viable 'transgenic' humans would yield success by the end of the year.

* * *

When Bob returned home from work, Anna May's nose was buried in a report she had found in her grandmother's trunk.

"Have you eaten anything today?" he asked.

She held up one finger as a request to give her a minute, and Bob went into the kitchen to retrieve a Bud Light from the refrigerator.

Sitting down at his computer, he logged on and downloaded his email. The usual—a dozen or so political tirades from his friend John Johnston, eight jokes from Pete Jensen, and new pictures of cats from Woody Williams. Phil Kenley sent new pictures of his latest grandchild and a dirty joke arrived from a co-worker. An Outlook reminder popped up informing him of a dentist appointment next Tuesday.

Anna May arose from her work, sat in his lap, put her arms around him and kissed him. "How was your day?" she asked.

"Typical Friday," he answered. "Everybody mysteriously disappeared around lunchtime and took off to the local watering holes."

"You didn't go with them?"

"Not today," he said. "I had a ton of crap to go through after being out of the office for two weeks. I'll finish up on Monday. How was yours? What did you find out?"

Anna May tilted her head, pursed her lips, and squinted her eyes. "Something was going on they didn't want made public, I'm sure about that."

"You mean public to everybody, or public within their own little group?"

"I'd say 'most definitely' to the first question, and 'most probably' to the last.

"During the first year, they were able to chemically synthe-size a bacterial genome and successfully transplanted the gene of one bacterium into another. Then they combined the two steps. Starting with a digital code from the computer, they built the chromosome from four bottles of chemicals, assembled it in yeast and transplanted it into a recipient bacterial cell."

She stopped and stared at him. "Did you understand one word of what I just said?"

"Not a damn thing," he laughed. "But I get hot when you shower me with scientific mumbo-jumbo."

"Oh, is that it?" she purred. "Shall we go right now?"

"Later," he snickered. "Lay some more of that scientific stuff on me."

"You're kidding?"

"No, for real. I'm very curious what you found out."

"Well, the teams didn't create a synthetic genome from scratch."

"They didn't?"

"No, but it's clear that was their ultimate goal. Instead, they copied an existing genome from the simple bacterium...Mycoplasma mycoides."

"Aha, the plot thickens," he joked.

"Yes," she said. "They wrote out its entire genetic code in a digital computer file."

"Now, we're getting into my area. How many bytes?"

"Bytes? We're talking megabytes here, computer guy...adenine, cytosine, guanine and thymine...the building blocks of DNA."

"You don't say?" Bob acted as if he was taking it all in.

"They translated the data into many small pieces of chemical DNA," she made a sewing motion with her hands, "stitching all that DNA together until they had a synthetic copy of the entire genome, booted up the new cells and produced daughter cells through replication..."

"You mean DNA does that too?"

"More than a billion," she said.

"Now you've lost me completely. One digit I can handle, but when you add nine zeros to it, I'm in the wrong apartment."

"Don't worry. It's probably sitting in a freezer somewhere waiting for regeneration."

"Okay, cut to the chase. Did they create synthetic life, or not?"

"I'd hesitate to call it *life*, but they did remove fourteen genes from the original M. mycoides, and they did give it a new name … JCVI-syn1.0, and Gran's notes say they embedded DNA sequences to identify the synthetic genome from the natural one."

"I'd love to see that kid on his first day in the first grade. 'Hi, my name's JCVI,' whatever you said, 'what's yours'?' I hope they taught the poor thing how to fight."

"Leave it to you to make something funny out of it." She laughed.

"You know, Dr. Frankenstein assembled a few body parts, shot it full of electricity, and the damn thing tried to kill him. There's no telling where this might lead."

"Well, right now, I'd like you to lead me to dinner."

Chapter Five
The American from Pakistan

The Democratic People's Republic of Korea might as well have been situated on a planet in another universe. With total isolation from other counties, it remained the world's most secretive society and was the only holdout for a pure communistic environment. Whereas China and Russia showed signs of rising capitalistic tendencies, North Korea did not.

Kim Il-sung, the country's founder, has enforced the philosophy of Juche, a state in which it would remain an isolated, independent, self-sustained nation, capable of surviving totally on its own. There was the flaw. Without the resources needed to feed its own people, the country relied on foreign aid despite its desire to remain self-sufficient.

In 2002, North Korea reactivated a nuclear reactor and expelled international inspectors. Four years later, they successfully tested a nuclear weapon and alarm bells went off around the world. Prompted by increasing food shortages, the country agreed to shut down its main reactor in exchange for food and supplies. But talks between North Korea, the US, China, Japan, South Korea and Russia failed, and the communists reneged.

New ways would have to be found to control its food shortage situation.

Kim Jong-il's death in December of 2011 brought hope that his son Kim Jong-un would free the innocent captives being held in the Korean prisons or at least end the somewhat contested *three generations rule* (yeonjwaje) that Kim Il-sung's supposedly imposed in 1972, but he did not.

* * *

Hussein Mehraj Khan, a Pakistani-American from Boston, stood at the edge of the frozen Tumen River on the border between China and North Korea. He was twenty-eight years of age and until recently, had been an English teacher in Seoul.

He obtained a visa to visit China and made his way by train to the village of Sanhezhen and hiked toward the North Korean city of Hoeryong. Soldiers of the Korean People's Army stopped him before he reached the border.

He produced a paper written in the Korean Language of Chosŏnmal saying he had come for a meeting with Kim Jong-un to discuss human rights violations. He was immediately arrested and taken to No. 22, Hoeryong Camp Kwan-li-so, a political penal-labor colony in northeastern Korea, one of the two main types of punishment facilities in the DPRK.

The camp had been modeled in the Stalinist tradition of a Gulag. Soviet architectural engineers had assisted the North Koreans in the construction of their prisons.

He was stripped naked and thrown into a filthy cell measuring five-feet in height, five-feet in width and five-feet long; one specifically designed to prevent a prisoner from completely lying down or standing up. He was fed once a day—a small, round bit of ground corn and a few cabbage leaves. In addition, he feasted on ants, roaches, spiders and small snakes that were unfortunate enough to venture within his grasp.

Near death, three weeks later, he was pulled from his cell. The muscles in his legs and arms had atrophied. The pain was indescribable, but rumors circulated of his unusual tenacity. Over the next three months, he was beaten, starved and publicly humiliated. During torture sessions, he appeared indifferent, apathetic, and unconcerned. When he was allowed to sleep, he slept head to toe with other prisoners on a cold concrete floor. Yet still, his stubbornness remained unshakable. It didn't take long before stories about the unusually defiant detainee reached the ears of Kim Bong Hwa.

Hussein Mehraj Khan stood shackled beside a garbage can of recently aborted babies—most of them dead, but a few were still alive with purple mouths and yellow eyes that blinked at him. He showed no reaction.

Hussein was thirty pounds lighter than when he first arrived at the prison. At 174 centimeters, he was five centimeters taller than the average man of his heritage. His roots went back to Afghanistan and his lineage was Tajik. He had dark hair and dark eyes, light brown skin and would be classed as an Alpine-Caucasian. He showed scars on his body from recent beatings, but his eyes revealed no apparent distress. He was obviously one tough son-of-a-bitch.

Kim Bong Hwa pointed to a cage that occupied the middle of the lab. It measured 244 centimeters square and some 300 centimeters high. There was a small cot, a sink and a toilet.

"Put the prisoner there," he said to the guards. Hussein cut his eyes from Kim Bong Hwa to the cell and then back again. The guards did as they were instructed. The Pakistani offered no resistance whatsoever.

"See that he gets a meal of rice and fish," he added.

Compared to the environment from where he was taken, to Hussein, his new cell must have resembled the penthouse at the Fairmont Battery Wharf in Boston.

Kim Bong Hwa pulled a lab-stool across the floor, sat a safe distance away from the bars, and appraised his newest specimen.

"What's your full name?" the geneticist said.

Hussein studied his jailer carefully. He saw before him a man of about thirty, clean shaven, slightly smaller than himself, and obviously well fed, yet Kim Bong Hwa's question provoked no response.

"I understand you are an American...is that so?" Hussein took note the man was speaking in perfect English, with a thick Korean accent, yet he still held his tongue.

Kim Bong Hwa sighed. "My friend," he continued. "You and I will be working together here in my laboratory for some time. If you cooperate as instructed, I will make your stay as pleasant as possible. If you misbehave, your stay will not be so pleasant. Your defiance is what interests me, so no matter what is going through your mind at the moment, let me assure you, there is no escape from this room."

He continued to stare into the dark eyes of the man in the cell. "We are located in a room, one-hundred-fifty meters beneath a bunker. There is no way out of this laboratory except through that door," he pointed, and Hussein's eyes followed. "If you attempt to leave, there are guards stationed on the other side who have been given specific instructions to take you back to the old cell with your playmates," he said. "Do you under-stand me, Hussein?"

The Pakistani nodded.

"Good," Kim Bong Hwa smiled. "Now I will give you food and you will rest. Tomorrow we will begin our work."

There was a knock on the door and a guard entered with the

food the scientist had ordered. The soldier opened the door to the cell and set a tray near the entrance. The prisoner retrieved it, returned to his cot and began to eat voraciously.

* * *

"I need your help," Anna May said.

Bob chewed his steak, swallowed, and then nodded.

"I need to get a look at the package the CIA is holding on *The Ladder Project*."

Bob looked astonished. "My group has no direct line of communications with the CIA, baby. I work for the FBI, remember?"

"Can you call them for me?"

"I don't think they'll talk to me without a directive from higher-up."

"Well, can you get that?"

"I'll talk to Otsuka. That's the best I can do. What do you expect to find out that you don't already know?" *Charlene Otsuka was Bob's immediate superior.*

"I've only studied it from Gran's perspective. There's probably a lot of information being held by the CIA that might confirm or dispel what we already know."

"And if it's true?"

"Then, I think I'd better tell them what I know."

Anna May was merely a few months old when her parents were killed trying to land a small Cessna airplane in a storm over the Rocky Mountains. Anna May's father was an excellent pilot, but investigators ruled it was most likely an unexpected downdraft that pushed the two-seater airplane into the mountains as they were approaching the Loveland Colorado Regional Airport.

Later that night, Anna May tried to think back as far as she could remember. Diane was a wonderful parent and Anna May missed her terribly. She wondered what her real mother was like. She had some pictures of her parents, but she found it difficult to get a feeling for who they were as people and what kind of parents they might have become.

Diane had spoken of her biological mother as a child. She had been much smaller than Anna May, and her grandmother assumed Anna May probably got most of her genes from her dad.

Her dad had stood six-foot four in his stocking feet and drove a truck for a local delivery outfit. Diane had objected to her mother marrying him because neither of them had made good marks in school. She wanted her granddaughter to have better, but what grandparent doesn't think about how their grandchild could have had better?

Anna May pondered what Diane would have thought about Bob. Bob had a pretty good education, and he wasn't dumb by any means, but she suspected Diane would have preferred she marry someone in her own field. She didn't think being a computer guy for the FBI would have impressed her grand-mother at all.

In his teen years, Bob Cook was already a Class A hacker. The remarkable thing is that Bob was an expert at retrieving data from a hard drive that had been demolished by almost any kind of computer virus. Most common computer viruses used the same basic algorithms to do their dirty work, varying only in design. By the age of twelve, Bob was cracking into his friend's contaminated data and freeing them from their digital prisons.

Bob's dad was a policeman, and he learned the difference between good and evil at an early age. He never used what he had learned as a weapon, only as a healer. When he graduated from the university with a master's degree in computer science, he immediately applied to the FBI, and after a thorough background check he was hired. Bob was a nerd.

But Bob was everything Anna May wanted. He was handsome, energetic, and he put up with her. Those were the three most important things as far as Anna May was concerned.

Diane never talked about why she didn't continue to work after *The Ladder*. They were never rich, but she always had everything she needed—the best schools, good clothes and nice friends. The money they lived on had to come from somewhere.

When Diane died, she left her a quarter-million dollars that came from an insurance policy. Anna May had never touched the money in the bank. She didn't need to. Each month, she received a check for $6,000 she used for her personal needs. It came from some retirement fund Diane had invested in before Anna May was born. Bob's salary covered most of the other living expenses, but even without Bob's money, she would have been okay.

Occasionally she would treat herself to an extravagance, but it wasn't very often. A piece of nice furniture, a new outfit, a trip to the spa—she never wanted for anything.

After she earned her PhD, within six months, she already had a job offer with a starting salary of $120,000. Barring any unforeseen circumstances, she felt she was set for life.

* * *

Special Agent in Charge, Charlene Otsuka, welcomed Bob Cook into her office located in the Southern California Field Office of the Federal Bureau of Investigation in downtown Los Angeles.

"Coffee?" she offered.

Charlene was a trim woman, about forty-five. Mr. Otsuka owned a shipping company in Long Beach and the couple married twenty years before, two years after Charlene was assigned to the Los Angeles field office. She had short blonde hair and was dressed in a dark, blue business suit. Rumor had it Otsuka had been FBI since the day she was born.

"I just had a cup," Bob answered. "But thanks for the offer."

"What's this about, Agent Cook?" Charlene was always on top of things and at the moment, she was quite busy. She was overseeing the mainland end of an investigation with the Honolulu field office, involving a large marijuana operation recently uncovered near the Hanalei National Wildlife Refuge, south of Princeville, on the Island of Kauai.

"You've met my girlfriend, Anna May Lee haven't you?"

"Oh, yes, you introduced her to me at the Christmas party last year. Is this about her?"

"You may not remember, but Anna May is wrapping up her PhD studies in molecular biology at the University."

"Yes, I think I remember you mentioning that when you introduced us. How's her progress?"

"She's waiting on her defense." Bob bit his bottom lip and dropped his eyes to the floor. He wasn't sure as to how his request would be received.

"Forty-five years ago, her grandmother, Diane Walters, was apparently working on a secret CIA project involving the creation of artificial life."

"She told you this?"

"She has the research papers of her grandmother, Agent Otsuka. I've read some of them myself. They're the real thing."

"Go on," she said.

"Her co-worker, a man by the name of Harry Robinson, had reason to believe that the project involved some action to eliminate the human race and create a new, more docile race to inhabit the Earth."

Charlene's eyes widened. "That sounds more than a little strange to me, Bob."

"To us too. Apparently, it upset him to the point of taking his own life."

"When was that?"

"A few weeks before the project was scrapped in 1968."

"They ended the project after his suicide," Charlene asked.

"Yes, ma'am."

She leaned in toward him. "Okay, continue."

"While we were on vacation, she received an anonymous message through Twitter that a man by the name of Kim Bong Hwa, who she knew of from a thesis he wrote while attending Caltech ..."

"That's where she studied, correct?"

"Yes, ma'am. And the message said he had made a break-through in evolution research."

Referring to her notes, Charlene asked, "What does that have to do with the creation of artificial life?"

"It seems that in the middle of the project, the geneticists split up into two groups. Her grandmother and this Robinson man stayed in the group working toward the creation of life, and the other group began working on a way to end evolution."

"Christ," Charlene said. "This is getting a little over my head. Your girlfriend has reason to believe this Korean fellow... what was his name?"

"Kim Bong Hwa."

"Was he related to Kim Jong-il?"

"She thinks he's a nephew."

"So, she thinks this man Kim Bong Hwa may have somehow resurrected this project? Does it have a name?"

"*The Ladder Project* is what her grandmother called it. Anna May has reread her grandmother's material describing the research, and she believes the CIA has buried *The Ladder Project* somewhere in their archives. She asked me if I could ask you, to see if they will let her take a look at it."

"Do you think she is qualified to justify this allegation?"

"I believe she is...yes, ma'am."

"I can't make this request without speaking with her, Agent Cook. After I talk to her, if I deem it appropriate, I'll try to feel them out. When can you bring her in?"

"Whenever it's convenient for you."

Charlene checked the appointment schedule on her computer. "How about Thursday at 10 a.m.?"

Chapter Six
The Turning Point

At their next meeting, Chung-hee Kyung showed a vast improvement in his appearance. He wore a flowered, aloha shirt, tan slacks, and black, wing-tipped shoes.

For the meeting, Colonel Hager had arranged a private room at the 'Korea House' in Seoul. It had a small room off the courtyard which provided privacy.

Through a window looking out into the courtyard, one could observe Korean dancers performing Ahbakmu, the ivory clappers dance, for an audience of tourists.

The meal was served by waitresses clad in *hanbok*, the traditional Korean dress. Chung-hee found the food a bit less spicy than he preferred in his new diet, but he seemed to enjoy it.

Dong-sun spoke to Chung-hee in Korean. "How are you adjusting to Seoul?" he asked.

"I like McDonalds," the boy answered. "Pretty cheap. Life is good here, if you don't get run-down by an autocar," he added.

"Yes," Dong-sun agreed. "People really do drive on the side-walks here. You have to always be on your guard. There are no traffic laws in the city, only suggestions," he chuckled. "Better you should avoid the streets and travel by subway...if you don't mind the soot.

"Have you found a yogwon?" Dong-sun asked, using the Korean word for temporary apartment.

"Yes," Chung-hee Kyung replied.

"Is it a nice one?"

Chung-hee shrugged. "It has a condom machine," he laughed. "And mommy-ajuma cleans my room once a week."

After a glass or two of okroju, a distilled liquor produced in Gyeonggi-do, the men got down to business.

Dong-sun began, "We would like you to tell us everything you can remember about the prison where you were kept, specifically your recollections regarding the camp at Haengyong."

"What do you want to know?" Chung-hee asked.

"Everything you can remember about the buildings, the guards, the fences?"

"There are many buildings, long and wide that house around 50,000 prisoners."

"How did you come by this knowledge?"

"The guards talked, we listened. After several years, you are able to put the pieces together."

"Go on."

"The prisoners live in brutal conditions of hard labor and semi-starvation. We received only enough food to sustain life. Everyone there is very skinny, as I was when I escaped.

"The entire prison is surrounded by barb-wire fences," Chung-hee added.

"How tall?"

"Three, four, seven meters high in some places, and they are electrified."

"What voltage?"

"As much as three...maybe four-thousand volts. Just touching one means certain death."

"How about the living areas?"

"You mean, where I stayed?"

"In general," Dong-sun said.

"They have closed compounds for villages of single persons and fenced-in villages for the families of the prisoners...parents, grandparents and children, sometimes grandchildren of the accused families...all must be punished for the prisoner's violations.

"There was a carving over the prison guards' headquarters that read 'Factionalist or enemies of class, whoever they are, their seed must be eliminated through three generations.'

"Some prisoners are allowed to marry and have children. My mother and father were exceptions. They were allowed to have sex but not marry. I have always wondered, what was the purpose?"

"To create the next generation, I suppose," Dong-sun suggested.

"Many prisoners starve unless their families send extra food for them to eat."

"How did you survive?"

"I was fortunate enough to be taken into the hills for hard-labor. We would catch insects and snakes when the guards were not looking. That's how many of us managed to stay alive.

"People are picked up and thrown into prisons without trials or even being able to face their accusers. Then they are tortured until they have told the whereabouts of their families and anyone else they are associated with.

"Everybody talks. The torture is so brutal you will tell them anything they want to know. One time I was tortured to tell of my mother and brother's attempted escape. I didn't even know enough to lie about it. They wouldn't stop until they thought you would die. Then they would take you to the infirmary and make you well until you were able to be tortured again. I was lucky my mother and brother were executed before I had to go back."

There was a pause in the conversation as the waitress came around to see if they needed anything. Chung-hee Kyung asked for another serving of rice and more vegetables. He appeared to know his way around a pair of chopsticks. He noticed other diners staring at him.

"In prison, you eat when you can, where you can, and as much as you can. It will take time for my body to become accustomed to having a full stomach."

"How does one go about getting into Camp 22 without being noticed?" Dong-sun continued.

"Getting in is no problem...getting out is impossible."

"I mean, getting in without being arrested."

"I guess you'd have to work there."

"Is there any other way?" Dong-sun paused. "Think Chung-hee. Is there any other way to get into Camp 22?"

Chung-hee Kyung thought for a minute. "One time an old man sneaked in to see his son. He was there for several days before a guard questioned him. They hung him the same day."

"How did he manage to get in?"

"Once a week, a railcar comes in through a fence delivering supplies. They said he got in by riding under the car, lying over the rods."

Chung-hee looked at Hager and then back at Dong-sun. "Hey, you crazy bastards aren't thinking of breaking into Camp 22...are you?"

"We would like you to take us there," Dong-sun said.

The boy swallowed hard. He stared at Dong-sun. He couldn't believe what he was hearing. "Back to Camp 22?" he said. "That would be insane. You'd be lucky to survive the trip, much less to get into the camp."

"We could fly to within five miles of the camp and walk the rest of the way... If you can pull it off, we'll pay you thirty-million won."

"No, you're crazy," Chung-hee Kyung insisted. He wanted to flee. He started looking for a way to get out of the room. Hager poured the boy another glass of okroju.

"Easy, Chung-hee. We're just talking here," Dong-sun said.

"You're serious, aren't you?" he gasped. "But why?" he stuttered. "What the hell you want to go to Camp 22 for?"

"There's someone in there we want to get out," Dong-sun answered.

"Oh, that's perfect," the boy scoffed. "Even if you're successful in getting into the camp, you plan on finding one prisoner in 50,000 and then just walking out of there with him?"

"We know it's going to be difficult, Chung-hee. But think about it," he paused. "Thirty-million won. You will be one of the richest men in Seoul when we get back."

"When we get back? When we get back?" he repeated. "We won't be coming back. How can I spend all that money with my intestines spread out all over the DPRK?"

Chung-hee Kyung thought for a minute about the ramifications of *not* doing it. What his life would likely become without the money he'd been getting from Hager and Dong-sun. What kind of life would that be?

In the capitalistic nation of South Korea, life would be

miserable without money, but never as bad as life in the camp. No, he would take his chances staying in Seoul—but he already had a taste of that kind of life. Begging for money, stealing enough to eat, treated like the filthy animal he was when he first arrived. He began to calm down, reached over and grabbed the bottle of okroju and poured himself another drink.

* * *

Kim Bong Hwa held the prepared, blood sample taken from the subject and added cold ethanol. It had previously been vortexed in a solution of sodium acetate. Since DNA is insoluble in alcohol, by spinning it in a centrifuge, he would separate the DNA and remove any salts that had been introduced in an earlier step. He switched on the machine, saw that it spun up to 15,000 rpm and went back to his desk.

Hussein Mehraj Khan sat in his cell with his back against the bars. He had not so much as uttered one word since his arrival, but he followed Kim Bong Hwa's movements with his eyes. This irritated the scientist somewhat, but he endured the prisoner's gaze in the interest of science. Till now, the Pakistani had cooperated fully with his demands. He didn't want to do anything that would change that.

Previously, Kim Bong Hwa had extracted samples of DNA from selected detainees displaying various characteristics—violence, insanity, docility, compliance, and so on. He would compare the agarose gel samples to that of the Pakistani's and apply those to a graph he had already started.

A Cray XT5 Jaguar supercomputer, recently smuggled in from Bangkok made his work a lot easier. Just as a molecular biologist would compare the DNA sequence of a horse to a gazelle, he would compare the Pakistani's DNA to other subjects and isolate the chromosomes that made this remarkable specimen what he was.

The lights flickered in his lab and the diesel-powered Kohler generator sprang to life. He cursed as he remembered his days in the lab at Caltech where the reservoir of electricity was infinite. Kim Bong Hwa reached over and rebooted his terminal. At CIA headquarters in Langley, Virginia, down the hall from KRYP-TOS, a red LED pulsed at a steady rhythm.

* * *

Anna May sat before Special Agent Charlene Otsuka. Intimidated to be sure, she tried not to show it. After giving her presentation, she sat down and waited for Charlene's reaction.

"Why do you feel this is a matter of national security?" Otsuka said.

"I guess my prospective on this situation might be a bit more focused than others," she replied. "While other children were learning their A-B-C's, I was reading my grandmother's research papers."

"You must be quite intelligent."

"I had a good teacher."

Otsuka picked up a pencil, tapped the eraser end on her desk, lifted it and rolled it in her fingers. "Genetic biology is a little bit above my pay grade, Ms. Lee." She paused. "I was going to say, I should probably get an expert in here to take a look at this, but going over your resume, I don't think anyone in the agency would be better qualified."

Anna May tried not to let her pride show. Rather, she remained silent and kept her gaze fixed on Charlene.

"Would you mind waiting outside while I make a phone call?"

Anna May rose from her chair, exited the room, and closed the door behind her. Seated near the reception desk in the front of Charlene's office Anna May received a buzz on her cell phone.

"How goes it?" Bob said.

"She's calling somebody. I'm in her lobby."

"How about *Joan's on Third* for lunch?"

"Pricey."

"You're worth it."

"Call and see if we can get terrace seating. It's a pretty day. I want to enjoy it."

"Will do, love you," Bob said as he disconnected.

Anna May had already decided she liked Charlene Otsuka, a lot. She was nothing like Bob had described. She wondered if it would be appropriate for them to become friends, given her relationship to Bob and all.

Fifteen minutes later, the secretary ushered Anna May back into Charlene's office.

"They don't claim to know *anything* about a so-called *The Ladder Project*."

Anna May raised her brow and tilted her head.

"Just sit tight. I've dealt with these people before. My guess is they gave me the stock answer. If they *do* have *The Ladder Project* on ice, in less than ten minutes I'll get a call. Curiosity killed the cat," she chuckled. "If not, then we can assume they never heard of it."

Charlene's phone rang less than ten seconds after she stopped talking. Charlene raised the finger of one hand and picked up the receiver with her other hand.

"Um hmm..." pause. "Um hmm... I have the granddaughter

of Diane Walker in my office as we speak. Um hmm... Um hmm... Will do." She hung up the phone and threw Anna May an astonished look.

"What?" Anna May started.

"Catnip," Charlene replied.

Chapter Seven
Meeting at the CIA

T he Central Intelligence Agency arguably was the most advanced military, scientific, and technological research center on the planet. Through the agency's information gathering activities, their main function was to furnish the military arm of the government, through the President, the intelligence it needed to carry out their operations. Honestly, the only thing that prevented foreign belligerents from being completely expunged was politics.

After failing in 1953 to conquer the US-backed Republic of South Korea (ROK), located in the southern half of the Korean peninsula, through state propaganda, the government of North Korea demonized the United States as the ultimate threat to its social system and molded political, economic and military policies around the core ideological objective of the eventual unification of Korea under Pyongyang's control. Likewise, the United States rated North Korea high on its 'top ten list' of America's most dangerous adversaries.

Having successfully survived for sixty-two years as a perpetual threat to the west, like Germany and Japan in World

War II, and more recently Iraq and Iran, the Democratic People's Republic of North Korea had maintained ridiculous delusions of grandeur.

Even though the United States had always possessed the firepower necessary to wipe North Korea from the face of the Earth, the high probability of China and Russia coming to the small country's aid stayed their hand.

Learned political scientists around the world believed all along a showdown between the two political powers was inevitable; but no politician in the American camp wanted the confrontation to occur during their watch. Understandably, any new or perceived threats from the DPRK drew serious attention from the CIA.

Unlike most government buildings in the area, made from quarried limestone with massive white columns, some with wide steps that rose one or two stories above the ground, the CIA building and its landscaped lawns resembled a well-kept college campus.

Located in Langley, Virginia, it was situated on a 258-acre tract of land located a mere eight miles from downtown Washington, DC. Anna May Lee and Charlene Otsuka passed through the impressive portal at the main entrance and entered the building.

The granite CIA seal, measuring sixteen feet in diameter, with its eagle, shield and sixteen-point star was set in the floor of the lobby and greeted them as they walked over it.

The Memorial Wall with 102 stars commemorated the CIA officers who had made the ultimate sacrifice. Directly beneath the stars, a glass encased 'Book of Honor' listed the names of sixty-three officers who died while serving their country. The names of the other thirty-nine remained a secret—even in death.

First and foremost, the purpose of the CIA was to act as an

intelligence gathering agency and had no authority inside the borders of the United States. The agency was often hated and despised in many parts of the world because, when authorized by the bureaucracy that controlled it, it was quite proficient at performing its work with surgical precision.

The two ladies entered a large conference room and sat before a group of men who were obviously not there for a social visit. Each person introduced him or herself, going around the table in a counterclockwise direction and beginning with the chairman.

Everyone present had a folder which included among other things Anna May's resume and credentials, copies of all the documents from Diane Walter's trunk, and Kim Bong Hwa's thesis, which had been acquired with one phone call from Charlene Otsuka to the science department of the California Institute of Technology.

The Chairman appeared to be a man in his mid-forties. He wore a blue suit, white shirt, and black tie. There was graying at his temples, and he possessed a commanding presence that screamed, 'I'm in charge'.

"Young lady," the chairman began, addressing Anna May, "what makes you believe this Kim Bong Hwa individual is working on the same project described in your grandmother's notes?"

"I only had a strong suspicion when I approached Agent Otsuka with my idea, but after she was able to acquire Kim Bong Hwa's thesis and after I had the opportunity to study it carefully, that suspicion turned into an absolute certainty."

"Can you elaborate?"

"There are entirely too many coincidences. If you read Kim Bong Hwa's thesis, you will see it coincides with the actual events that occurred during *The Ladder Project*. It's as if he copied it directly from the information in my grandmother's notes. I have come to the conclusion he was privy to information about *The Ladder Project* when he authored his paper.

"I know my grandmother didn't give him *her* notes, and *I* certainly didn't give them to him, so it drew me to the conclusion that someone else must have. I think the individual was a man named Harry Swanson, who I believe may have worked as an informant for the CIA. Further, I believe something happen that made him turn and sell a copy of her notes to the North Korean government, and Kim Bong Hwa used them to complete his thesis."

The chairman addressed the other participants. "Have we been able to locate this...Swanson fellow?"

"Swanson died three months ago. He left no family," one of the other members of the conference stated.

"Hmph," the Chairman grunted. "And your suggestion, Ms. Lee?"

"No one knows my grandmother's notes better than I, and if I had a chance to fill in a few gaps, I think I can prove my hypothesis."

"What leads you to believe the CIA is in possession of this...*The Ladder Project*?"

"Mr. Chairman, if you don't have it...that scares the devil out of me."

"Agent Otsuka," the chairman said, turning his attention to Charlene. "Have you had a chance to do a complete background check on Ms. Lee?"

"Yes, I have, sir, and her friend Bob Cook is an employee of the Los Angeles field office. That's how it came to our attention."

"I suppose Agent Cook has a top-secret security clearance?"

"That's correct, Mr. Chairman."

The chairman made eye contact with the other members of the conference. He leaned forward. "Would you two ladies mind waiting in the foyer? We'll have you back in a few minutes."

* * *

Sitting in the lobby as instructed, Anna May asked Charlene, "How do you read these people?"

"We'll have to wait and see. This is the most secretive operation in the government. I've been here on several occasions, and I've never been able to guess what's going through their heads."

"I think they're worried."

"The CIA never gets worried...unless some Congressional oversight committee calls them on the carpet for one thing or another. It takes someone with a great deal of intestinal fortitude to put up with their day-to-day meddling." Charlene paused. "The world is not always what it appears to be, Anna May."

Charlene sat on one end of a sofa, crossed her legs and pointed to an armchair positioned at her left and angled toward her at forty-five degrees. Charlene was old enough to be her mother, but on the trip from LA, Anna May had gotten to know here as more of a friend.

"So, what does Anna May Lee do when she's not working on molecular biology problems?"

"I listen to jazz mostly, but usually while I'm seated in front of a computer." She laughed.

"It's none of my business, and you don't have to answer this, but I can't help wonder if you and Bob have talked about getting married and having a family."

"I don't think I'd make a very good mother," Anna May said.

"Do you want a family?"

"I don't know. You know, Charlene, I've been a scientist my entire life. I never knew my mother and father. They died in a plane crash a few weeks after I was born. My grandmother raised me. She never worked while I was growing up, and she had all the time in the world to spend with me. She kept me away from the television and kept me interested in all things scientific. I miss her a great deal."

"I'll bet you do."

"You know, Bob was the first real boyfriend I ever had."

"Really?" Charlene threw her a surprised look. "You're a lovely girl, Anna May. I would think you grew up beating suitors off with a stick."

"Oh, it's not that. I knew boys...went to a few dances, a movie here and there, birthday parties, down to the beach...you know. But they were so...*stupid*."

Charlene laughed out loud. "It's going be kind of hard for a man to possess the same number of brain cells as you," she chuckled.

"No, I didn't mean I want them to be geniuses. But my God, Charlene, men my age are so immature. Who wants to go to the beach and lie around and drink beer all the time?"

"Bob's sharp," Charlene said. "I think he has a promising career ahead of him.

"Well, there you have it. With Bob's career and my career, I don't think it would be fair to have children. I'd never be able to do what Gran did for me. I'm not ready to give up my work just yet."

"You like it, don't you?"

"I'm absorbed in it, Charlene. By the time I was fifteen I was rehearsing for the Nobel Prize presentation.

One thing I really like about Bob is he understands my dedication to my work. He never complains, well, not out loud." She grinned. "Sometimes when he wants to talk and I'm busy he grumbles a little bit, but then he gets a book or turns on the TV or finds something else to do. I don't think anyone else would put up with my constant preoccupation with science like Bob does.

"Hey, you know everything there is to know about me. How about you? Tell me about your family."

"Well, I've got two boys and one grandchild."

"Both of them married?"

"Oh no...Charles is twenty-two, but Jimmy is just starting the 3rd grade."

"That's quite a stretch."

"Jimmy was an accident."

"I'll bet you love him best."

"Why do you say that?"

"I think little accidents always turn out better than grandiose plans." Anna May laughed.

"That's a strange statement, coming from a geneticist."

"That's what evolution is all about. Tens of millions of little accidents over billions of years is what made you...*YOU*. Most of my discoveries are accidents. Education put me into a place where I can recognize them when they appear. I'll bet you're proud of both boys," she added.

"Charles has been a little bit of a disappointment."

"Really?"

"He quit college in his sophomore year and married a secretary for a building contractor. Oh, we love them both, I don't mean otherwise, and they gave us an adorable granddaughter.

But when Jimmy came along, I've tried to not make the same mistakes I made with Charles."

"What mistakes?"

"I don't know. That's what I worry about the most."

"I think parents can give their children good values while they're young," Anna May said. "But unless you can control their lives all the way through college, which you can't, of course, the way they turn out has a lot more to do with their environment away from home that it does from what they learn from parents."

"You're wise beyond your years, Anna May."

"What were your parents like?" Anna May said.

"My dad was a general in the Air Force and my mom was a stay-at-home mom. I had a younger brother. His name is Francis. After watching him grow up, I vowed never to name either of my sons Francis," she said with a chuckle.

"When I was a little girl, we had TV to keep us occupied. My father said they didn't have a television until he was thirteen. When he was a kid they had bicycles, fishing, hunting and dances. I have no idea what my grandparents did for relaxation growing up."

"They're ready for you now," a secretary said as she approached the two ladies.

"Well, here we go," Charlene remarked as the two women gathered their briefcases and returned to the conference room.

Pastries and coffee were served, and a curtain had been opened uncovering a gray screen at the far end of the conference room. After the servers had vacated the room, everyone took their seats.

"Ms. Lee," the chairman said. "We are in agreement that we would like you to have access to the documents you requested.

But first, you will need to sign the CIA Security Oath." He slid a document over to Anna May.

"Read it carefully before you sign it, Ms. Lee. Violating the terms can have severe consequences."

Anna May took her time reading the paper, lifted the pen, and signed it. Then she slid it back to the chairman. He examined it carefully, countersigned it, and put it in a folder. The lights were dimmed, and a presentation began to play on the screen. The chairman spoke as the slides changed.

"On May 25, 1961, President Kennedy announced to Congress our intention to put a man on the moon by the end of the decade, many government projects were created to support that goal.

The Ladder Project was only one of hundreds. The project assembled a research team to create a simple life form that would be able to sustain itself on the lunar surface. The first astronauts to walk on the moon would place it there.

"Dr. Peter Langstrum was picked as the team leader and twenty of the best molecular-biologists in the country were chosen to work with him.

"The only weak link was a man by the name of Mark Todd. He had strong connections with the Kennedy family and his appointment as Project Manager was some sort of payback for his parent's support in getting John Kennedy elected President in 1960.

"The research team was split into ten groups of two researchers each. Your grandmother, Diane Walters, was paired with Harry Robinson and the project went into full operation in January of 1965, a little over a year after the Kennedy assassination.

"The following year, the military had President Lyndon Johnson in their pockets. The Vietnam War was raging and losing the support of the American people, and of Congress. The military needed a way to bring the war to a successful conclusion before the whole thing fell apart and we would have been forced to admit defeat, give the country of South Vietnam to the communists and turn tail and come home.

"Knowing they would not be able to acquire funding for a new project, a directive came down from the Johnson administration to split the teams and put half of them on a course to invent a biological or chemical weapon to destroy the North Vietnamese army and end the war.

"The teams continued to operate in isolation, and what Dr. Robinson, driven by rumors and half-truths managed to gather from casual conversations with other researchers, caused him to come to the conclusion his peers were engaged in an action by which the entire world's population could be destroyed and replaced with a more docile race.

"Dr. Robinson erroneously theorized that the aim of the second group was to put an end to evolution. A possibility that he knew was in the team's power to accomplish. He believed they were unwittingly engineering a mass extinction event.

"Langstrum was under strict orders to keep the purpose of the second team a secret. Robinson seemed concerned that by playing with the normal progress of evolution, a chain reaction might occur that would somehow stop evolution in its tracks and inhibit an organism's ability to mutate against biological attacks. He believed a new strain of something as benign as the common cold might start a pandemic that could not be checked. The more Dr. Langstrum attempted to put Robinson off the hunt, the more convinced Robinson was *The Ladder Project* was some kind of dooms-day operation.

"After Todd was attacked in his apartment by an operative of a foreign power, probably a female Korean spy; without thinking, the CIA liaison officer by the name of Major Edward Blevins made the mistake of ordering a lockdown of the entire team. In Robinson's confused state, it was all that was needed to convince him his suspicions were valid.

"When he committed suicide, it hit the CIA like a bombshell and when the White House found out about it, afraid that word could leak out to the American people, the project was abruptly ended, the teams were paid off, forced to sign oaths of secrecy, and went on their way. The files regarding *The Ladder Project* were buried in the archives of the CIA and the director at the time thought that would be the end of it.

"Approximately two years ago, it came to the attention of the agency that a nephew of Kim Jong-il by the name of Kim Bong Hwa had embarked on a plan to interrupt evolution. Red flags went up in the scientific community and after acquiring a copy of Kim Bong Hwa's research papers from Cal-tech, we ordered the university to remove him from their roles and to disavow any knowledge of him ever being a student there.

"A request by Agent Otsuka for Kim Bong Hwa's thesis shook the university to its very foundation and, thinking they had no choice, they complied with the request and released a copy to the FBI."

"Yes," Charlene said. "I made the request before my first meeting with Ms. Lee."

"When Agent Otsuka contacted us regarding *The Ladder Project*," the chairman continued, "we ordered *The Ladder Project* documents retrieved from the archives and thanks to your inquiry, that's how we were able to link Kim Bong Hwa to *The Ladder Project*."

"So you already knew everything before we arrived here today," Anna May said.

"Not exactly," the chairman replied. "We knew this Kim

Bong Hwa fellow might be trying to follow the path of the second group, but we could use some help in figuring out how he might go about it.

"Before we go any further, Ms. Lee, we need to know if you would consider working with the CIA to help us solve this problem."

"You're offering me a job?"

He nodded.

"Doing what?"

"We can't tell you that until we're satisfied you're on board."

Anna May was in shock. She had come to Washington to get a small glimpse of *The Ladder Project*, more out of curiosity than anything else, and her whole future was playing out in front of her.

"On one condition," Anna May said.

"And that would be?"

"I would like to work with my friend Bob Cook."

"He's the computer specialists that is also your boyfriend?"

"Yes, sir."

"That would depend on whether Agent Otsuka is willing to put him on leave until the project is over."

"It could be arranged, Mr. Chairman," Otsuka said.

"Agreed," the chairman said. "Thank you, Agent Otsuka. You may be excused now."

"Charlene knew instinctively they were about to get into the area of 'Need To Know'. She wished Anna May luck, thanked the men and women in the room, and started for the door.

"Just a minute, sir," Anna May said. "May I be allowed to have a few words with Agent Otsuka before she goes?"

"Certainly," he said. "I'll call a two-hour lunch break and we'll reconvene at, uh...shall we say, 14:00 hours?"

The meeting broke up, and Anna May followed Charlene out of the room.

"They just threw you out, Charlene. How could they be so rude?"

"You're working for the CIA now, honey. They weren't being rude. That's just how the business is run. They are going to talk about something where I can't possibly be of any help. There is no need for me to be there."

"But they took Bob away from you. I took Bob away from you. I haven't even talked to Bob. He may not want to do this."

"Anna May, listen to me," Charlene took the girl's hands in hers. "This is serious stuff, honey. Your country needs you. I'm very proud of you. This is a chance of a lifetime. I'll explain it to Bob. Unless I miss my guess, he'll be overjoyed to get an opportunity like this. I think he's getting a little board with the law and order gig anyway. A little mystery and espionage will be right up his alley, and he loves you very much. I'm sure he would be miserable back in LA with you here in Washington."

"But what if he says no?"

"He won't, baby. I'm sure of it. Say, I'll tell you what. I know a great place for lunch. It's not very far from here, and you have nearly two hours before your next meeting. What say I treat you to a fantastic lunch and we can get in some more girl talk before you have to come back here?"

Chapter Eight
First Day at the Company

K im Bong Hwa studied his computer terminal as his prisoner watched him from behind the bars of his cell. He had examined scores of genomes trying to ascertain the difference between that of his captor and other DNA samples he had harvested. Compared to others of his sex, he could find no difference. He rubbed his eyes and searched through his notes, looking for anything that might tell him what made his prisoner so different.

He began to wonder if a person's personality could be manipulated through their DNA or was everyone born the same, and what they learned in their formative years was what made them who they are? But that didn't make sense either. No, it had to be more than that. He had seen too many cases where identical twins, raised in identical environments, had completely different personalities. The more he thought of it, the more he was convinced. Changes in the cells, maybe too small to be detected had a great deal to do with the disposition of the individual and the evidence had to lie within the cells of every human subject. By God, he was going to find it if it meant sacrificing every prisoner in every camp in the DPRK.

Hussein Mehraj Kahn studied the scientist and continued to remain silent. Kim Bong Hwa felt his gaze and wondered what was going on in the Pakistani-American's mind. *Why doesn't he speak?* Kim Bong Hwa thought. He had studied the interrogator's reports. The prisoner had refused to speak even when tortured. *Was he even capable of speech? Was he missing the gene of violence, and if so, where the hell was it?*

He supposed his subject's tendency toward stubbornness and self-determination could at least be partially attributed to his treatment after his initial arrival at Camp 22, but he wondered what he might have been like before...in Pakistan, how he adjusted to American society while living in the United States, and how he had changed in the culture he most recently lived in. He knew he had come from South Korea, because papers taken from him on his arrival indicated he had a recent address there. He needed to find a way to open a line of communications between the prisoner and himself and he felt a mounting anxiety to moving forward with his research.

He was also aware of the value of his prisoner. By the time he had acquired previous subjects, they had already been severely injured and too terrified to allow him to draw any worthwhile conclusions as to their true character. This man had been in captivity for only a short time before he acquired him, and he showed no signs of psychological damage like the others. He knew he might never get another chance to obtain such an individual for his experiments.

After several days, he decided to embark on a new experiment. He would release the prisoner from his cell and let him have the supervised run of the lab.

* * *

Paul Roberts was too young to be the Chief Information Officer of the CIA. At any rate, that was Anna May's appraisal when she first met him. However, looks can be deceiving. Roberts was a captain in the Marines. Like Bob, he had an education in computer science and after only a few minutes she realized she had underestimated him.

He had sandy hair, an infectious smile, wore a tan military uniform and tan, khaki pants.

"I thought all you guys wore suits," she said.

"Disappointed?"

"No...just surprised."

"Us peons haven't worn suits in here for twenty years." He laughed.

"Afraid you'll be shot as a spy," she joked.

Ignoring her last remark, he slipped his passkey into a slide on a heavy glass door and invited her in.

"They'll bring your pass key down before the end of the day," he assured her.

They walked into a hallway that made a slight turn that prevented passersby from viewing the computer screens that lined the room. *Must be at least twenty-five in this room alone*, she thought.

"You're computer-savvy?" he asked.

"I make out," she answered.

"I suppose they told you you're not allowed to talk about your work outside of this facility...unless you're authorized to do so by a superior."

He ushered her into his office. It was surprisingly sparse. A desk, a file cabinet, a telephone and two guest chairs in front of a government-issue desk.

"I'm not sure yet who my superiors are," she said.

"I don't think it'll be me," he said. "They'll probably bring you in as a civilian contractor, in which case you'll be assigned to Jim Atkins."

"When do I meet *him*?"

"He should be back from the Puzzle Palace any minute now."

"The Puzzle Palace?"

"That's what we call the Pentagon around here."

She smiled.

"Microbiology is a hot ticket at the moment. All around the world, our enemies are dropping their nuclear programs and moving into weapons-grade, germ warfare. I take it you're one of the best in your field."

"I don't know if I'm allowed to talk about it."

"You learn fast," he said.

"I'm trying," she replied.

"Well, can you answer this question?"

"If I can," she replied.

"Coffee, tea or...?" Paul rose from his seat as a six-foot tall Marine major stopped at his door.

"At ease, Captain," the Marine said. "You must be Miss Lee," he smiled as he extended his hand. "I'm Major Jim Atkins."

"It's my pleasure," she replied. "You can call me Anna May."

"Have you been waiting long?"

"No, I just arrived a few minutes ago and Captain Roberts here was kind enough to entertain me."

"Have you been scheduled for SCI indoctrination?"

"I don't even know what that is, Major."

"It's a one-day class on maintaining the secrets involving national security."

"No, sir, not that I know of," she answered.

"Well, for now, don't take anything from inside outside with you. When you passed through those doors," he pointed in the direction of the exit, "everything you hear or see in this office, you will automatically assume is a closely guarded secret. Come with me," he instructed.

"Thank you, Captain Roberts," she said to Paul as she began to follow Major Atkins down a series of hallways that made up a labyrinth so confusing she decided she would need a map to find her way out.

The Major's office was a bit more elaborate than Paul's. There were trophies along the walls and pictures of racehorses of various sizes and colors. Anna May took a seat in one of the large leather chairs that faced the Marine's desk.

"I will give you a rundown of the landscape of our operation, so you'll have a better understanding going in," he said.

Anna May straightened her dress and took a notepad out of her briefcase.

"The notebook is fine," the Major said, "but just be sure you leave it within these walls when you leave at night."

"Yes, sir."

"How much do you know about this Kim Bong Hwa fellow?"

"I've read his thesis. It seemed benign enough, that is...until I recognized it appeared to have come from my grandmother's notes. Then it got *really* interesting."

"*The Ladder Project*?" he said.

"Yes, sir."

The Major pressed his thumb to his lips and lowered his head. Then, he locked his gaze on the young girl. "You know *The Ladder Project* started off as a study to see if a life-form could be created to survive on the lunar surface?

"I do now, but until it was explained to me, I assumed it was something else."

"Yeah, well, so did Kim Bong Hwa and his crazy uncle. Apparently, they thought it could be used to wipe out the human race outside the DPRK."

"When did you come to that conclusion, Major?"

"About a year ago, we got a communiqué from a mole in the North Korean government stating as much. That's when we got involved."

"So, my contact with the FBI wasn't really necessary."

"On the contrary. We've been looking for someone...anyone that had a connection to the project, but it appeared all of them were deceased, except for a Major Blevins and a guy named Harry Swanson. Swanson killed himself before we could get the opportunity to question him. Blevins is eighty-eight years old now, and his memory is not with him anymore.

"We tracked your grandmother Diane to your mother, but when we found out she was deceased as well, it never occurred to us to look at you."

"*The Ladder Project* was my *Alice in Wonderland*." Anna May smiled. "I grew up reading about it, but I didn't know a great deal about the second group until after Gran died.

"Her co-worker, Dr. Robinson, was fascinated with the Cambrian Explosion. He thought the second group was about to create a mass-extinction event and, without knowing it, wipe out the entire human race," she paused. "So, you think that's what Kim Bong Hwa's trying to do?"

"Most of my micro-biologists say it's impossible. What do you think?"

"I don't think Kim Bong Hwa's that smart. If he was, he would understand the finality of a successful experiment."

"But do you think it can be done?"

"I believe that sooner or later, mankind will find one way or another to destroy itself."

"But do you think it's possible?"

"Yes, sir, I think it's possible."

"How do you see it playing out?"

"The mutation would have to be delivered."

"How?"

"He'd probably choose something simple, like a common-cold virus as the carrier. We already know that DNA possesses sequences that instruct the immune system to distinguish 'foreign' from 'self'. If you could construct one that would contain the reverse instructions, you could command the body to destroy itself. There are several scenarios that could be played out."

"Do you believe the DPRK has the resources to accomplish the task?"

"Probably not all of it. They might need a little help," she said.

"What kind of help?"

"Well, it would require a sophisticated distribution network. They would need to unleash the virus carrying the package world-wide. If I knew the direction he was going, I could give you a better answer."

"We may be able to help you there, Miss Lee."

"You have a crystal ball or something?" She laughed.

"We may have something even better than that. We have..." The phone on Major Atkins' desk started ringing.

* * *

Colonel Hager arrived in Songham City at a place where the 707th Special Mission Battalion was going through training.

Dong-sun and Chung-hee accompanied him.

The 707th was part of the Republic of Korea's Army Special Warfare Command and originally formed after the Munich Massacre as a prelude to suspected terrorism during the 1988 Olympics held on South Korean soil.

Chung-hee would go through an eight-week crash-course in basic infantry, parachuting, rappelling and mountain warfare, martial arts, firearms and demolition.

Chung-hee was expected to endure a training exercise where only 10% succeeded in graduating. Chung-hee however, had a much stronger motivation.

At first, the idea frightened him. After all, he had endured horrible atrocities at the hands of his North Korean tormentors. In the camps, he had been a helpless child, and he feared his captors; but this was different. As he began to entertain the idea of revenge, he started to become more enthusiastic. With the excellent training he had been promised, *he* would be the aggressor this time.

He would also have a marked advantage upon completion. The guards that operated Camp 22 tended to be overweight, overfed, and overconfident. Major-General Dong-sun was to serve as his trainer.

Dong-sun had warned him it would be tough. This caused Chung-hee Kyung to laugh out loud. *Dong-sun*, he thought, *has no idea what tough was*. He doubted anyone did. Six months in South Korea had allowed him to put on some weight, but most of that weight had come in the form of muscle. He had also acquired something else—hate—a boiling hatred for his North Korean tormentors. His opinion of his mother and brother had also changed. At least they had attempted to escape from the hell of the DPRK and he felt some family pride in that.

Chung-hee Kyung sailed through the first week of training

with little effort. Then it began to get hard. He started to appreciate what he was learning. He realized how, by overcoming his fear and becoming the aggressor, he built up self-confidence and determination.

In the third week, three additional, fully trained South Korean Special Forces soldiers, joined with Dong-sun and himself to make up a team of five men.

In-su, the most experienced who had won a Silver Star fighting with the U.S. Marines in Afghanistan, Jin-sang, the tallest man Chung-hee Kyung had ever seen and the one with the best personality of the group, and Kwang-ho, a little dynamo that could run circles around the other three.

For the first time, Chung-hee Kyung had friends. Men that would fight alongside him, and if necessary, give their lives for his. The concept was very strange to him. In the camp, every man was considered a potential enemy. He spent long hours in his bunk at night trying to understand this new kind of relationship, where a team made up a complete organism, and no single man in the team was greater than the team itself. He decided that he rather liked the idea, but nevertheless, he would remain cautious.

The only thing that Chung-hee Kyung didn't understand is that they were going into North Korea to rescue someone very important and not to kick-ass. He wondered if he would be able to resist the urge to serve up some pay-back. Chung-hee wasn't the only one concerned. He had company. Dong-sun too wondered if that was going to turn out to be a problem. But the boy was doing so well in his training he tried not to dwell on the thought.

Chapter Nine
The Roommate

Using a foreign dialect Anna May never heard before, much less understood, Major Atkins jabbered away endlessly in a heated telephone conversation.

Ten minutes into the call, an attractive redheaded girl appeared. She knelt down near Anna May's chair and whispered in a soft voice, "Hi, miss I'm Bambi Marshall. What say I buy you a cup of coffee 'til Major Jim gets off the phone?"

Taking Bambi's cue, Anna May quickly rose from her chair and followed the young lady out of the office. The two women stopped in the hall.

Bambi was a stunning girl, twenty-five years old, with fair skin and bright green eyes. Her business suit and shoes appeared to be straight out of Hollywood and made Anna May think of one of those James Bond women from the '007 movies made in the sixties. Her manner of speaking was sweet, syrupy, and delivered with a thick southern accent.

"I apologize for us havin' to meet this way, hon...but I'm the major's secretary. And when I put that call through, I just knew somebody needed to come to your rescue... poor thing. Shoot, that man may be on the phone for hours. Let's you and me go up to the dinin' hall and get some refreshments. How 'bout that?"

"You sure it'll be alright?" Anna May said, glancing over her shoulder.

"Now, don't you fret none, sweety. I reckon you won't be seein' him again for quite a spell."

"Okay," Anna May replied. "I could use a cup about now." She paused before she asked the next question. "Say, you're from somewhere down South, aren't you?"

"Lanta," Bambi replied. "How'd you guess?"

Anna May squinted her eyes, trying to make out what the girl just said.

"Georja?" Bambi ended a great deal of her sentences with a question—the polite, southern way of adding...'Ya'll understand now?' to a statement.

"Aha, not too many people have that accent where I come from. It's quite attractive though...I like it."

"My brother, Harley? He told me when I got up here to 'Warshinton', they'd most likely chase me off with a stick. But it makes a body smile, you know what I mean? I like to make people grin...don't you? Some people accuse me of workin' at it, but it's the real me, I swear. Here we are," she added as she accompanied Anna May Lee into the dining hall.

The cafeteria was a large room capable of seating 1,400 people for lunch, but at this time of day no one appeared to be eating. On one side of the room there was a wide canteen that offered everything from a simple cup of coffee to a complete, prepared meal, shrink-wrapped and ready for the microwave.

"Back home, my daddy, he farms peanuts ... he was in the

Vietnam War, you know? I declare, how he managed with that one arm ..."

How is it possible I would know that? Anna May silently thought. She was about to get her first lesson in southern conversation. *Does it always start with genealogy?* She was wondering.

"My sister, Sue? She teaches third grade, and Harley, my brother? He married a gal from Alabama way? That one didn't last long," Bambi said, shaking her pretty head. "You know, she popped out two babies in thirteen months? They weren't twins neither. *Sumpin* must have been workin' there fer sure.

"Then he divorced her and married Cousin Libby. It's okay though, cuz she was our grandmother's brother's daughter, so it don't count. She wuz about his age though. Her mamma and daddy started late? I figure she was a mistake."

Anna May was being indoctrinated into Bambi Marshall's past, one relative at a time.

Finally, there was a break in the conversation and Anna May jumped at the opportunity to get a word in edge-wise. "You know who I am?" she said.

"Course I do," the girl said. "I processed your dossier. How d'ya'll like DC?"

"It's frightening," she replied.

"Ahhh...You'll get used to it. There's a lot of interestin' stuff to see 'round here."

There was something about Bambi that made Anna May feel happy all over. Kind of like when one gets their first puppy, and they have to hold him at arm's length to keep him from planting doggy-kisses all over their face. It was that kind of feeling, as if she had suddenly become the most important person in the world. She liked it...very much.

"I'm especially looking forward to the Air and Space Museum. Ever since I was a little girl I've wanted to go there."

"Oh, sweetie, they got so much interestin' junk over there... lemme tell ya." Bambi moved in close like she was about to disclose some dark secret. "There's this one exhibit where they fly you through the universe in 3-D. Heck, I ain't never even been as far as LA, and I felt like I done been shot through space on a rocket."

Anna May laughed in spite of all her confusion.

"They got missiles and airplanes hanging from the ceiling. They even got a lunar landin' module that... Say, have ya'll found a place to stay?"

So this is what southern conversation was like, Anna May thought. *First, it starts with genealogy, then a lesson on your surroundings, and ends with a question.* Anna May was all ears.

"They put me up at the Watergate, Anna May responded. I've got this tiny room that's ancient. It has a TV from the stone-age and the frame is held together with electrical tape." She laughed.

"That's a scream," Bambi said. "I've got to get you out of there...Say, you know what? I've got an apartment about a mile from the office with a spare bedroom. The landlord? He's real nice, you know? But his wife is a lil' bit crabby," she said, wrinkling her brow. Lowering her voice to a whisper, she added, "I think she's goin' through the change. You know what I mean?"

Anna May cocked her head, trying earnestly to catch every word.

"Ah, you know how women get when they go over the hill and start goin' down the other side?" Bambi went on without skipping so much as a beat. "Anyway, my roommate? Her name was Linda. She moved out last week after she was reassigned to

London. Can you imagine that? Goin' to London this time of year? Musta forced her, you know? A body'd have to be nuts to do such a thing on purpose."

Bambi moved in closer for another secret. "She had this weird boyfriend, you know? He looked like Billy in that reality show, Parker's Cove? You know the one where they put those people up in space and watch 'em tryin' to figure out how to use the bathroom and get along with one-another? Say, why don't you just move in with me 'til you find your own place?"

"That's awfully kind of you, Bambi. I'd really like to get out of that hotel, but it would only be for a few nights. Are you sure I wouldn't be a bother?"

"Heck no, girl, we'll have us a good ole time, and I'll tell you sumpin' else. I'll take you 'round to all the sites over the weekend."

"I think Bob...he's my roommate, will be coming up on Friday."

"That's even better. The more the merrier, I always say. We can make it a foursome. Tom, he's my fiancée, and a staffer for this senator from Louisiana, you know? Now that man's a real hoot, I'll tell ya, girl. He's a descendent of that governor they called Uncle Earl? What does Bob do anyway?"

"He's an F.B.I. agent out in LA, but I hope he'll be working here with me at the CIA."

"Honey, my apartment is *big*." She tried to let the word 'big' stretch out into infinity. "It's plenty big enough for everybody."

Anna May studied on what she meant by *everybody*.

"You and your friend Bob are both welcome to stay in the other half as long as ya'll like. We can share the kitchen and the livin' room. I won't even know ya'll are there. We can split the rent and utilities 'til ya'll find a place of your own."

"Well, I don't know …"

"Awe, come on Anna May, it'll be fun."

"Well, okay, we can try it. I'll have to talk it over with Bob."

"You guys are gonna have to get acquainted with the area anyhow, and we've got a great bunch of friends and I'm sure ya'll-a fit right in."

Just then Bambi's cell phone rang. She could tell by the ringtone playing the *Star Spangle Banner* it was her boss.

"Yes, sir. Uh-huh…will do." Turning to Anna May she said, "Now if that don't beat all? I could'a told you that was gonna happen when I sent that call in to Major Jim.. before? Why, I just knew that man would be on another airplane within the hour. Let's go get your stuff, sugar-pie," she said excitedly. "Then I'll introduce you to the D.C. night life."

When they arrived at Anna May's room at the Watergate, it didn't take but a few minutes to gather up Anna May's suitcase and throw it in the back of Bambi's Honda Accord.

The Congressional Bar & Grill was crowded when the girls walked through the front door. They worked their way through the crowd and headed for a table where six other women were seated. Everybody was talking at once.

"Listen up, ya'll," Bambi announced. "I got a new best friend I want ya'll to meet."

In a flash of silence, the gaggle of women stopped in mid-sentences and turned to look at Bambi.

"Ya'll, this here is Anna May Lee, from LA. She's a new *white coat* at the company. Anna May, I want you to meet Barbara, Sally…" she pointed around the table, "Betty, Sue, Libby and Keisha."

"Hi, Anna May," they all said in perfect unison.

Then the girls picked up their conversations from where

they stopped and there was a cacophony of non-stop chattering as Bambi pulled up two chairs and motioned for Anna May to sit.

"What can I get you from the bar, sweetie?"

"I'll just have a glass of Chablis."

"Well, you just sit right there, honey, and I'll be back directly," said Bambi, who turned and left Anna May seated by herself.

She never had been good at starting up conversations with strangers. At any rate, it didn't appear there was a lull in any of the conversations where she could jump in. So, Anna May just sat still and listened until Bambi returned with the drinks.

Bambi told Anna May all the girls around the table worked at the CIA in some capacity or another. Individually, they had their own group of friends, but when all of them got together, almost every day after work, non-CIA friends were not invited to attend.

They never discussed what might be misconstrued as 'sensitive subjects' in public. There was always the chance of an infiltration from bad actors outside the company, especially journalists, and no one wanted to take a chance that even one, simple, innocent remark might tempt one of those snoopy news hounds into connecting something that was said with some project they were involved in. Then, it might end up on the front page of the Washington Post. No one wanted to be called up in front of security to explain an innocent remark.

After two more glasses of Chablis and an hour of listening to Bambi relate the rest of her life story, Bambi announced, "Girls, we got to be headin' on out now."

Like a planned military movement, the girls stopped chattering and told Anna May how nice it was to meet her, and how they looked forward to seeing her again. As they went back to their chattering, Bambi and Anna May made their exit.

There was a chill in the air with an occasional raindrop now and again. After a quick bite at a fast-food establishment, the girls started for Bambi's apartment. The streets were wet, and Bambi drove like it was a sport, weaving in and out of traffic, like Jeff Gordon at Talladega.

"Wow, you really know how to drive in this traffic," Anna May said. But she said it in a way that she hoped Bambi would take it as a request to slow down.

Careening around a corner and just missing a BMW, with its rear-end sticking a little too far away from the curb, Bambi said, "I heard traffic in LA was a lot worse than this."

"We're not used to driving in the rain out there, I guess."

"Well, we're here," Bambi announced as she came to a stop and slid into one of several open parking spots available on K Street.

The building was an impressive brownstone with concrete steps that formed an 'L' shape up to the front door. The architecture suggested the 1800s, and you had to look carefully to recognize the differences between the individual structures.

Some had little trees in front, others stairs that went straight up from the street. There were similar ornate designs above every door, but no two in a row were the same color. The front of Bambi's apartment was tan colored. The building to the right was gray, and the one on the left was pink, but at night, the colors were a bit difficult to distinguish apart.

There was a light in a yellow globe hanging over the front entrance that desperately needed cleaning... or changing. The light flickered just a tiny bit as they ascended the steps with Anna May's suitcase and a box of things she had neglected to pack.

Bambi inserted her key into the lock of the front door and stepped inside, holding the door open for her new roommate. They ascended carpeted stairs with what looked like a hand-carved rail and balusters. When they reached the second floor, they made a slight right turn and entered the apartment into a large living room.

The walls were eggshell-colored and the floors were hard-wood with throw rugs placed in strategic places. The main room had a couch and recliner lounge across from a 42" flat panel TV on one end, and a dining room-kitchen combination on the other. It was tastefully decorated with modern art renderings that Anna May was certain didn't come from Bambi's private collection. Illumination was provided by exposed wiring and lights suspended from the ceiling. There were windows along the backside of the living room that looked out over more houses to the east.

To the right was Bambi's bedroom. The bed could be seen through a set of French doors, and another set of doors on the left opened into the guest bedroom. There were full baths adjoining each bedroom.

After unpacking her clothes, Anna May took a quick shower, wrapped herself in a terrycloth robe and joined Bambi in the living room. A rerun of Seinfeld was playing on the television and sit-coms always gave Anna May a sick stomach, so she politely excused herself by saying the time-change had thrown off her internal clock and she needed to go to bed early.

She pulled the French doors closed, climbed into bed, and turned on her laptop. When Windows finished loading, Bob was waiting for her in IM.

"How it going, babe? " he wrote.

"Okay, I guess."

"When you coming back?"

"Haven't you heard?"

"Heard what? "

"They want me to stay."

"For how long?"

"I only accepted the offer on one condition."

"And that was ????"

"That you could come too. We'd better not talk about it online. Otsuka will tell you about it in the morning."

"Why can't we talk about it now?"

"I'm still a little concerned about security. I had to sign a bunch of papers."

"What kind of papers?"

Anna May didn't answer.

"Calling..."

Anna May's iPhone rang. She grabbed it and pressed the answer button.

"Why can't we talk about it now?" Bob said.

"If I could answer that, we could talk about it." She laughed. "I just may be here for a while," she added.

"Okay, okay, I get it. Tomorrow then. Can you at least tell me about your day? Where are you staying?"

"I'm staying with an employee of the company for a few days."

"A he or a she?"

"A she. She's a crazy nut from Atlanta. I think you two will get along," she said.

"What did you guys do?"

"She introduced me to some of her friends...all girls. Then we grabbed a burger at McDonald's and came straight home."

"Okay, I've got to get back on this report. It needs to be submitted in the morning. I love you."

"I love you too."

"I'll be on-line if you need me."

"Bye-bye."

"Bye."

Anna May plugged her phone in to re-charge and turned out the light.

Chapter Ten
The Gulag Banquet

At this point, one might be curious as to how Kim Bong Hwa's family ties into this story. Well, it doesn't, actually. Kim Jong-il was most certainly his uncle, but the nephew had only met him once in his life—at Kim Il-sung's residence when Kim Bong Hwa was only five years old.

He obtained his lab mainly by a request made to his paternal grandmother, who passed the request along to the 'Dear Leader' on his behalf. Kim Il-sung often handed out jobs as a result of family requests. It served as insurance that relatives did not meddle in his affairs of state.

Insanity within the Kim family line was common knowledge, but no one dared talk about it, for it would mean a one-way ticket to the gulag where a person would learn first-hand what insanity was all about.

With each of Kim Il-sung's descendants, a new psychotic element surfaced. While Kim Bong Hwa appeared to come from one of the more rational branches of the Kim family tree, he had his own quirks, to be sure. The main one being although he shared the same lack of regard for human life, if protecting someone gave rise to a stronger mania, one which made him feel superior to everyone around him, he would exercise compassion as long as it served his purpose. Kim Il-sung suffered from a severe case of paranoia and insecurity, as did the majority of the Kim line. After the need for superiority had been satisfied, the victim was just as likely to be tortured and/or exterminated as not.

To the last man and woman of the Kim family, the people of the DPRK were little more than tolerated vermin used to produce soldiers to expand and fortify what was often referred to as 'the fourth largest standing army in the world.' That would be tantamount to the tiny island of Samoa being the world leader in aerospace technology.

The leaders of the DPRK felt no more compassion toward their citizens than they would a common housefly or a crippled grasshopper. The Korean population existed to serve the government and produce soldiers, be it male or female, and that was the end of the story—not so much different from many species of the insect world.

Training in the Korean People's Army was especially brutal. Participation was compulsory to non-Kim-family members and many recruits died in the process of becoming soldiers in the *Inmin Gun*—a common name used to identify the KPA. Kim family members, on the other hand, were awarded high-ranking commissions and desk jobs. Nothing occurred within the KPA unless expressly ordered by Kim Jong-il. After the death of his father, Kim Il-sung, Kim Jong-il was the unquestionable master of his country.

The KPA was the primary instigator of the Korea War, (known behind the walls of the country as the 'Fatherland Liberation War') against the South Koreans in 1950s. As known outside of the country, it ended in an embarrassing loss for the North Koreans, but inside the country it was hailed as a successful and glorious victory against the Imperialists' forces of the United States of America, who "without provocation, had attempted to invade North Korea and destroy the 'peaceful' government of the North Korean people."

It had long been a matter of speculation as to whether the North Koreans possessed a substantial amount of fissionable material to produce more than one nuclear weapon, but the fact that they were pathological liars, militarily strong and impossible to reason with, was sufficient enough to keep western powers on their toes.

* * *

Hussein Mehraj Khan, the Pakistani-American who had been captured near the border in China, gazed through the opening of his cell. He rubbed his eyes. The door had been removed, and it appeared he would be able to walk freely out into the lab. His captor had given him an injection before he left the previous evening. He assumed it was to make him sleep. He had lost track of the days and the hours, as he was always being medicated. There were no windows or clocks in the room to mark the time of his imprisonment——only his captor's wristwatch, which the scientist glanced at continuously as if he expected it to take wing and fly away.

He studied Kim Bong Hwa, a shorter man and slightly older than himself. So far, he had treated him well, but he never seemed to give him enough to eat, or maybe it was a side-effect of all the drugs he had been given.

Kim Bong Hwa sat on the other side of the door, spectacles hung on the end of his nose, looking up and fiddling with the stem on his watch. "Geseki," he mumbled, followed by a loud "Shib seki."

He looked over at Hussein. "Good morning," he said in a cheerful voice. "North Korean merchandise can be quite troublesome at times." He smiled and strapped the watch to his wrist.

"Come and sit with me. I have ordered the morning meal and we shall eat and have a nice talk."

Driven by hunger, the prisoner arose from his bunk, stopped at the door and scanned the frame where the door had been, as if he wondered what had happened to it and expected it to suddenly reappear from out of nowhere.

"It's okay," Kim Bong Hwa assured him. "Come here and join me." He pointed to a comfortable chair beside his desk.

As Hussein stepped into the room, a surprised guard entered with a tray of food.

"It's okay, comrade. The prisoner is going to dine with me today."

The guard set the tray down and threw a disgusted sneer at Hussein. The prisoner, taking his seat in the proffered chair, ignored the guard's disdainful stare.

"How did you sleep, my friend?" the scientist said.

No reaction.

"Come, come, my friend. You must be hungry after your long rest. I only wanted us to have a nice conversation this morning."

* * *

So, it was morning, Hussein thought. It was the first time the Korean had attempted idle chat, and Hussein assumed he was up to something.

"You know it gets terribly lonely in this lab," he pointed his finger at Hussein. "And you haven't been very good company."

Hussein wanted to climb over the *buckethead's* desk and strangle the life out of his captor, but for the time being at least, he managed to control the urge.

"Don't be so surprised, my friend. You have been very kind in providing me with the samples I needed for our work, and I have given you so little in return. Won't you please allow me to reciprocate in kind?"

Remaining mute Hussein continued to stare at Kim Bong Hwa with his dark eyes. His mind was already running at full speed, planning an escape.

"Oh, very well," Kim Bong Hwa said. "I'll do the talking until you decide to say something. In the meantime, shall we eat?"

As Kim Bong Hwa uncovered two trays of food, the presentation made the Pakistani salivate. The meal consisted of the customary rice. Very few Korean meals were served without rice in one form or another. This one included lima beans and was accompanied by a bowl of kimchi jjigae...a stew made with fermented vegetables and tuna.

Hussein had suspected he was being poisoned with every meal, but he relaxed as soon as he saw the scientist take both men's portions from an identical source.

Hussein ate hungrily as Kim Bong Hwa spoke.

"We are about to embark on a marvelous play in which you are to be the main character," he began. "I am a microbiologist; you see...a doctor...and a graduate of one of the finest American universities in the United States of America. How long did you live in the States?"

The Pakistani held his tongue.

"No matter," he waved off the prisoner's silence. "You and I are extremely fortunate to have come together at this particular point in time. Sooner, and the opportunity to do our work would have not presented itself. Later, and it might have been too late.

"You see, for some time now I have been studying aggressive behavior in human beings and your case leads me to believe your hidden aggression can be treated. I only want to help you, my friend. Once this aggressive behavior has been conquered, you may go home with our blessings. But if you persist in this antisocial manner, I'm afraid you will have to remain a prisoner for quite some time." Stopping to study Hussein's reaction, he added, "You *would* like to leave and go back to South Korea, would you not?"

The Pakistani lowered his eyes for a moment, then looked back at Kim Bong Hwa and nodded, once.

"Then you will help me?" Kim Bong Hwa asked excitedly.

Hussein was torn between two mental states. In one, he had become a beaten man. He had had enough of this race of maniacs and would do whatever was required to get released. On the other hand, he saw himself as a man with remarkable resources and he would try with every fiber in his being to flee from his captors.

"Yes," he said.

"Good. Now, let's finish our delicious meal and then we can decide together how you can best assist me in solving our problem."

Kim Bong Hwa had no intention of helping Hussein, of course. Not one bit. His theory was that his prisoner's genome was hiding a specific gene that controlled aggression. Studies had been conducted on mice by his peers in America, suggesting the hidden gene made it impossible for the brain to produce the neurotransmitter nitric oxide, and in his opinion, nitric oxide was the key to the puzzle. If he could find the errant gene in the prisoner's DNA, he could synthesize the genome. The next step would be to detect the presence of the gene in all of humanity and eliminate those humans without it. He would use the absence of the gene in question to trigger an enzyme which would destroy the host's ability to mutate, introduce a killer virus and let nature take its course. It was a grand plan, and he was convinced he would succeed, gain the admiration of Kim Jong-un and the recognition he so desperately required.

* * *

Anna May heard Bambi in the kitchen. She looked over at the bedside table and the clock displayed 6:30, which was only 3:30 on the west coast. Because of the time change, she had tossed and turned until 3:00 a.m. trying to go to sleep. That meant she had only three hours and thirty minutes of actual sleeping time and she felt terrible.

She dragged her poor body out of the bed, and half-asleep tried to stand erect in the tub. After dropping the soap three times, she began to perk up, finished her shower, dried herself off, brushed her teeth, combed her hair, put on a nice dress, and trudged out into the kitchen.

"Good morning, sunshine," a perky Bambi Marshall greeted her.

"Coffee..." It was the only word Anna May could muster.

"You look tired, you poor thing. Didn't you sleep well?"

"Time change."

"You sure you feel alright?" Bambi said with concern.

"I will be. Just give me a minute to wake up," she answered.

Riding in the passenger's seat through early morning Washington D.C. traffic with Bambi Marshall at the wheel was all it took to pump up her blood pressure. By the time Bambi presented her identification at the front gate, her new roommate was wide awake.

When they arrived at Bambi's desk, there was a note:

Ms. Anna May Lee
SCI Indoctrination
08:00—Room3640.

Anna May looked at the clock—8:15. "Uh oh, I'm late."

When she arrived at the session, people were milling around, engaged in gossip and shop-talk. Anna May slipped in without being noticed.

The training session was on-line, and it was over by lunchtime. She assumed she must have passed because she received her badge, and she was able to leave the room without an escort. She was afraid she might miss her next appointment with Human Resources, so she decided to postpone lunch and hurried on over.

She was surprised to be interviewed by one of the women she met at the Congressional Bar and Grill who greeted her and helped her fill out the paperwork. She was back at Bambi's desk by 2:00.

"He's still not back," Bambi said, referring to Major Atkins. "But Captain Roberts said for you to come to his office as soon as you got here."

"How do I get there?"

"I'll take you there, honey," Bambi said, getting up from her chair. The two women walked briskly to Paul Robert's office. Bambi said she would find her at the end of the day, and Anna May walked into Paul's office alone.

"Good morning, Miss Lee. Have they been running you ragged today?"

"Kinda," she answered.

"It can be a little confusing around here for newcomers. It won't take you long before you know your way around.

"Come with me." He got up out of his chair and motioned for her to follow.

"I hear you're staying with Bambi," he said. "What do you think about her?"

"She's a piece of work." Anna May chuckled.

"Yes, Bambi is our main source of entertainment. Don't let it mislead you, though. I don't think this place would run without her greasing the wheels."

They stopped in front of a large semi-circular room with huge video-display terminals all along the walls. It reminded her of an I-Max theatre, only about five times wider. Paul inserted his passkey into the card reader and the door clicked open. He selected a terminal on the right-hand side of the room and sat down. Anna May took a seat in a chair beside him. He pulled up a satellite image of what appeared to be a collection of buildings on a barren landscape surrounded by mountains.

"You are looking at Kwan-li-so No. 22 in North Korea. This is where your buddy is."

Looking for something interesting to show her, he zoomed down into a crowd assembled in an area that resembled a schoolyard. She could make out three people tied to post on one side of the compound. The detail was remarkable. On the other side, there was a puff of smoke from three rifles. The bodies jerked and their heads fell forward.

Anna May didn't have to be told what she just witnessed.

"I'm sorry," Paul said. "I didn't know that was going to

happen." He switched off the monitor. "Are you okay, Miss Lee?" He grabbed her before she slipped from her chair.

When Anna May regained consciousness, she was lying on a cot and a nurse was checking her vital signs.

"Where am I?" she asked.

"You passed out," the nurse replied. "You're in the infirmary. Captain Roberts brought you in. How do you feel?"

"A little bit woozy, I didn't get much sleep last night, skipped breakfast...no lunch. I'll be okay."

"He said you passed out after viewing something."

"Oh, yes. I remember," she said.

"Do you have a family doctor?"

"Not here in Washington."

"Drink this," the nurse said as she gave her a cup of orange juice.

Anna May drained the contents and laid her head back down on the pillow.

"You rest here for a minute," she said, and went into her office to fill out the paperwork. A few minutes later, she came back into the room and saw Anna May sitting on the side of the cot.

"All better, now?"

"Yeah...a lot."

"I think you'd better have your blood-sugar checked," the nurse said.

Anna May moved into a chair and rested a little longer before she returned to Captain Robert's office.

"Are you okay?" he asked.

"Yeah, I'm fine now."

"Why don't you take the rest of the day to rest up?"

"No, I'm fine. I just needed a little glucose. Not enough sleep, and I didn't eat today."

"It wasn't from what you saw?"

"Could have triggered it, I suppose. But not to worry, I've seen worse than that on television." She paused for a second. "Was that a live scene I was looking at?"

"No, it's the middle of the night over there. It was a feed taken early this morning. We have a spy satellite that stays over North Korea twenty-four seven. We're watching all their known missile launch facilities for any unusual activity. If they get a bird in the air, we'll know about it before it leaves the pad."

"And what were we looking at?"

"It's Camp 22 near Haengyong. Kim Bong Hwa is working there in an underground bunker."

"How do you know that?"

"We arranged for the North Koreans to get their hands on a Cray XT5 Jaguar supercomputer. They took the bait and smuggled it in."

"Why?"

"It's our version of a Trojan Horse. They don't know it, but that machine was especially manufactured for them. It has a unique O/S and a little bit of hardware that allows us to hack into it without their knowing it. You won't actually be working on his computer...just copies of his data. It's a one-way portal. We can see him, but he can't see us. We keep a mirrored image of their data on our IBM Blue Jean. Every time one of their operators so much as touches a key on one of their terminals, we pick it up."

"Really?"

"Pretty cool, huh?"

"Amazing," she said. "So what do we know so far?"

"Your boy, Kim Bong Hwa has been a busy fellow, but most of what he is doing is crap. He keeps the machine running endless calculations. We think most of them are creating worthless data streams to shield his stupidity from his co-workers. Your main job will be to sort them out. Look for the relevant data and discard the rest."

"So, when do we get started?"

"Let's go take a look at your office."

Chapter Eleven
Anna May Goes to Work

W hen Anna May saw her office, she was quite pleased with her new surroundings. It had a nice view of the courtyard located three stories below a large window. Technicians had almost finished installing her workstation, and they explained to her how to use her pass-card to access the system. She was given a three-inch thick operating manual and instructed as to how she could contact the help desk for support.

There was a high-tech phone on her desk with a lot of multi-colored buttons she would have to learn how to use, a pen and pencil set, an empty filing cabinet, two upholstered office chairs and her name on the door read Dr. Anna May Lee, Ph.D. *Well, it will only be a few more weeks*, she thought. There was a large plastic palm in one corner of the room, and in another, an attractive hutch with glass doors to display various knick-knacks, pictures, and awards.

She was taking it all in when her telephone rang. Bob was on the line.

"Where were you?" he asked.

"When?" she replied.

"I called earlier and they said you were out."

"Oh, silly me. I didn't eat all day and I had a tiny fainting spell."

"Are you okay?" Bob sounded concerned.

"Oh, I'm fine. They just gave me a glass of orange juice and I stopped off at the canteen and bought a Snickers bar on the way back. That'll hold me 'til supper."

"Well, you gotta be sure and eat, baby."

"I will. Bambi and I'll get a quick bite on the way home, then we'll stop at the grocery store, and I'll pick up some fruit and junk. Say, did you talk to Otsuka?"

"Damn, what did you do to her?"

"Whatdaya mean?"

"She was actually civil to me."

"Well, whatdaya think?"

"She likes you."

"I mean, whatdaya think about the situation?"

"It's a done deal."

"Really?" Anna May was surprised. She had assumed it would take weeks.

"Was there any doubt?" Bob questioned.

"Okay, tell me...what's the deal?"

"I'll finish up a few details here and I'll see you on Friday. I get into Dulles International on Delta, Flight 203 at 10:00 p.m.. I'm on loan to the CIA until you're done, or I get called back, which she doubts will happen."

"That's odd."

"What's odd?"

"It's just odd that it was so easy. I figured there would be a lot of red tape."

"I don't know all the particulars yet, but I think this is

something really big, honey. You're a big wheel now...for the time being anyway. Enjoy it while you can."

"They've rolled out the red carpet. You know...I'm not so sure why."

"Meaning?"

"Meaning I'm not so sure I deserve all this attention."

"It's crazy, isn't it?"

"Whatdaya mean?"

"Just be careful, baby."

"Careful?"

"Yes, baby. Very careful. The CIA has a reputation of getting what they want regardless of who they have to go through to get it."

Anna May spent the remaining hour reading and familiarizing her way into the system. A virtual partition on the computer had been assigned for her use. Tomorrow she would begin to explore the virtual network connection called *The Ladder*.

At 5:30, Bambi showed up to take her to the apartment. Instead of going straight home, they went into the city and stopped at 'We, The Pizza' on Third at Pennsylvania for dinner. Anna May ordered a 16", *Forest Shroomin* pizza, and Bambi settled on two slices of Salami Pie.

"My stars, honey. Can ya'll eat all that?" Bambi said.

"I'm starving," Anna May answered. "I'll take home what's left and eat it later."

"You feelin' all better now?"

"Oh, I'm okay. I'm not used to going all day on an empty stomach, I guess." She decided to change the subject.

"How do you like working for Roberts?" Anna May said.

"I don't work for Paul, honey. I work for Major Atkins."

"Well, what do you think about him?"

"Jim?"

"No, Paul?"

"He's a damned flirt," Bambi stated.

"Is he married?"

"Married to the sweetest 'lil ole soccer mom you ever did see."

"How long have you known him?"

"I've been here two years, an' he was here when I started workin'."

"He says nice things about *you*."

"You be careful with that one, sweetie."

"You mean he's a problem?"

"I'll just say this. Don't bend over if he's standin' behind you." She laughed.

"That's the second time today someone's warned me to be careful."

"Really?"

"Yeah, Bob called today and pretty much said the same thing."

"Does he know Roberts?"

"No, he meant for me to be careful in general. I take it you're not Paul's biggest fan."

"I don't trust him no further than I can toss a cow."

"How about Major Atkins?"

"He's nice...a good boss...his wife is nice too. He seems devoted to her, but..."

"But what?"

"I think if I gave him the right sign, he'd be like all the rest."

"It sounds to me like the company is a hotbed of lecherous Don Juan's."

"Oh, no, I didn't mean it like that," she said and chuckled. "It's jus' nowadays...well...you know how men are?"

"Tell me about Tom."

"Well, lemme see. Tom's twenty-six, goin' on thirteen." She laughed. "Like I said, he's a staffer for a Louisiana senator. His family is involved in the fishing industry. I met him about three weeks after I started workin' here."

"Are you two serious?" Anna May wondered if Bambi could be serious about any man.

"Damn sure better be," Bambi grinned.

"How do you guys handle it? I mean, with both of you working in, I assume some pretty sensitive areas?"

"Oh, honey, Tom's got a top-secret clearance too. But we don't talk about work when we're together."

"Bambi, is there some kind of danger that goes with our jobs?"

"There's a certain amount of danger in everything, sweetie. Just don't get too loose with the wrong person."

"Like?"

"Like if some guy starts hittin' on you, jes' remember where you work. That pretty face might be after more than your body."

Anna May ate what she could of her pizza and ordered a to-go box to take the rest back to the apartment. They made a detour to the Chinatown Market over on H Street, where Anna May picked up some fruit, vegetables, eggs, bacon and milk—she wasn't going to leave for work on an empty stomach ever again.

Bambi was the kind of person that ate when and where she wanted to. There was nothing in the refrigerator but ice cream, beer, a bottle of white wine and a jug of cold water. Not one thing anybody could make breakfast out of.

That night, Bambi talked her roommate into watching an

old Jack Nicholson western on HBO, but she gave out after thirty minutes and excused herself to the bedroom.

Before she went to sleep, her thoughts drifted back to what Bambi had said about Paul Roberts. He was quite friendly and came across as a nice guy. He hadn't tried to hit on her or anything like that. But still, there was something about him that gave her reason for pause. She probably wouldn't have given it a second thought except for the look on her roommate's face when she talked about him. As she drifted off to sleep, she made the decision to stay on her guard when she was around him.

The morning sun streamed through Anna May's window and woke her up before the alarm was scheduled to go off. Her internal clock was still fighting to adjust to Eastern Standard Time. She threw on her terrycloth robe and ventured into the kitchen to make coffee. Bambi was still asleep, and she could hear her snoring through the partially cracked bedroom door.

She opened the refrigerator and took out a peach. It was as hard as an apple, and she had to slice it up in order to chew it. California peaches picked green and ripened on the truck as they made their way across the states left a lot to be desired. She regretted not picking up a box of cornflakes at the market. She made a mental note to rectify that situation on the way home that evening.

Bambi made her way into the kitchen at 6:15, poured herself a cup of coffee and took her place at the dinette next to Anna May.

"You never eat breakfast," Anna May asked.

"Never took up the habit, I guess. I'll get a sticky bun at the canteen when I get to work."

"How do you keep your figure?"

Bambi shrugged.

Anna May resisted the urge to give Bambi her lecture regarding healthy eating.

After she finished off her first cup of Maxwell House, Bambi said, "Hey, Tom's comin' by tonight. You wanna go with us to the Congressional Bar & Grill?"

"I really appreciate it, Bambi. But I think I'll stay at the apartment tonight and catch up on my PhD defense."

"When you going for that?"

"I have to fly back to L.A. at the end of the month."

"Then we'll have to call you Dr. Lee instead of Anna May."

"You can keep calling me Anna May, my dear. I'm not too excited about this 'doctor' business anyway."

"Well, you should be. You've worked hard for it."

Anna May let that statement slide and asked, "How far did you get in school, Bambi?"

"I have a master's in political science from L.S.U."

Anna May looked shocked. "What are you doing working as a secretary?"

"I originally wanted to be an agent, but they didn't have any openings. They said they'd hire me as a secretary 'til an agent position came up. I thought about going and applying to the Bureau, but heck, I always wanted to work for the CIA, so I decided to hang on there 'til somethin' more interestin' comes up."

"Why the CIA?"

"I want to travel...go to Europe, London, Rome, Germany...I don't wanna get stuck in the states." She looked at the clock. "We'd better get a move on, girl, or we'll be late again," she said as she set her empty cup in the sink.

Bambi still drove along the George Washington Memorial Parkway 'like the dickens', as Bambi would have said, but Anna

May was getting used to it, and her driving didn't bother her nearly as much that time. They pulled up to the gate at 7:55.

Anna May made her way to her office and met a young secretary in the hall.

"Golly, you're Dr. Lee, aren't you?" The girl had messy brown hair and a ponytail. A pencil was stuck over her left ear above horn-rimmed glasses. She looked every bit like a school librarian. She was struggling with a huge stack of papers.

"Not quite yet," Anna May answered. "Just call me Anna May."

"Pleased to make your acquaintance, Anna May...I'm sure," she said, managing a cute little curtsy.

"And who might you be?"

"Oh, sorry." She attempted to move her right hand out from under the stack of papers and caught them just as they started making their way to the floor, leaving Anna May's hand hovering in mid-air.

"Here, let me give you a hand with those." Anna May retrieved about half of the papers from the girl's arms and accepted her handshake.

"I'm Sally...Sally Gooden? I'm the gofer 'round here. You know, like anything you need help with jus' call on Sally...paper, envelopes, copying, mail...you know? Stuff like that? I'm a pretty good typist, but with computers and all, I don't get much call for that anymore."

"That's nice. How can I get in touch with you?"

"I'm on your phone. Miscellaneous, like M-I-S-C? Just press that button."

"Where do you want these?" Anna May said, holding out her share of Sally's papers.

"Oh, golly, right in here." Sally made a few steps into a small reception area about the size of a large walk-in closet. "Just put them here." She pushed some desk items over so Anna May could lay her stack down.

"I'll be sure and call you."

"Yeah, anytime, Dr. Lee...I mean Anna May. Golly. Thanks a bunch for helping out."

"My pleasure," Anna May assured her as she made her way to her office.

Sitting at her desk, she opened the manual the support team had given her and went through the steps to boot up her terminal and sign onto the system.

When she attempted to get into *The Ladder* folder, the system prompted her for another password. She looked through the manual, found the proper code, and typed the correct collection of numbers, characters and symbols ... thirteen in all. The sub-directories were sorted by date. She began with the first item and browsed through the files, reading each one in date order.

Kim Bong Hwa may have been a lot of things, but he kept an excellent diary. The first file was dated Monday, August 2, 2010, 12:00 p.m. She assumed it was the first day they brought the new system on-line, only two months after he had defended his PhD at Caltech.

For the first few months, he had followed Diane's notes regarding synthesizing genomes to create artificial life, but on November 17th he seemed to become more interested in Dr. Robinson's concerns regarding tampering with evolution. It was about that same time he began dabbling in horrific experiments on living subjects.

Anna May stopped at the door to Major Atkins' office and knocked.

"Good morning, Ms. Lee, how can I help you?" he asked.

"Major Atkins, could I get the full contents of *The Ladder Project*?"

"All of it?"

"Yes, sir. I'm trying to make sense of Kim Bong Hwa's notes and I need to check on a few things to determine what path he's following."

"I'll send a note down to archives and have them delivered to your office this afternoon. How do you like your new surroundings?"

"Better than I expected. The view is breathtaking."

"I thought you might like that," he said with an air of pride. "I picked it out myself. Did you meet Ms. Gooden?" he added.

"Oh, her? She's cute as a bug."

"Don't sell her short. She's an industrious little cuss, that one. If you need anything, start with her. If she can't put her hands on it, it doesn't exist. You and Bambi getting along okay?"

"I'm considering buying a car."

"She drives like a bat-outta-hell, doesn't she?" he said with a smile.

"You've ridden with her?" she asked.

"Just once," he answered.

"I wonder if everybody from Atlanta drives like Jeff Gordon."

"You think Jeff Gordon drives like that?" he asked.

"Good point," she laughed.

After Anna May returned to her office, Bambi stuck her head around Anna May's door. "Time for lunch, sweetie."

"Where we going?" Anna May said, grabbing her purse.

"I thought we'd head over to Reagan and zip 'round the runways." She grinned.

"He told you?" Anna May said with a look of disdain. "I

had him pegged all right. How can anybody get hired into the CIA that has such a big mouth?"

"Don't fret, darling. My drivin' is legendary 'round these parts.'"

For lunch, Bambi decided to take Anna May somewhere really special. She drove into the city, found a parking space in the Hotel George and took the elevator to *Bistro Bis* on E Street Northwest near Capitol Hill.

The interior was impressive, a very modern version of a French bistro with a warm, natural cherry interior. The full bar was graced with tall columns with fabulous fixtures and a soft, patterned tile floor. A magnificent glass wall offered a view into a busy kitchen. Anna May recognized several senators and congressional leaders she had seen on the news.

"This place must cost a fortune," Anna May started.

"Don't get your panties in a bunch, darling—my treat," Bambi joked.

A waiter directed them to a table elegantly set with expensive tableware, water glasses and ornate utensils arranged on crisp white tablecloths.

"Well then, you do the ordering, Miss Moneybags," she laughed. "I wouldn't have the slightest idea what's good here."

Bambi ordered two glasses of *Tattinger Brut* champagne and *Fricassée d'Escargot* for appetizers.

"You shouldn't spend so much money on me, honey," Anna May said, looking around. "This place must be where half the federal budget goes."

"Don't you fret, sugar. This here was Major Jim's idea. He's paying. You scared the fire out of him when you passed out. He wants to be sure you get fed good n' proper. After lunch, I want to take you over to meet a doctor friend of mine. Jim wants us to check out your blood sugar."

"I really don't need to do that," Anna May complained. "I can see my own doctor when I go back home to defend my thesis."

"Nonsense, girl. You're way too important to the company to let you go traipsing off to California without a checkup. No sweat...the company's paying for that too."

The waiter brought their drinks and snails, unfolded the napkins and offered them to the girls to place on their laps. He was tall, with black hair and a handsome physique and spoke with a slight, polite, French accent, 'Yes, Ma'am, No, Ma'am and 'As you like, Ma'am.'

"Now, where did you meet this fabulous man we're going to meet at the airport tomorrow night?"

"Oh, you don't need to trouble yourself, Bambi. I can manage."

"Tom and I are very excited about meeting Bob. But if ya'll don't want us to..."

"Oh, it's not that. I just hate to be a bother. You've been so nice to me and all. I would feel guilty about imposing on your time with Tom." Anna May wasn't accustomed to getting so much attention. She was beginning to feel like her life was being directed; but she had to admit, it was kind of nice to be treated like a VIP.

"Please. It's very important to me, you being new and all. We'll pick up Bob, take ya'll back to the apartment, and then you can have him all to yourself." Bambi was being rather insistent.

"Well...okay. If you're sure we won't be an imposition." Anna May gave in.

"Are you ladies ready to order?" the waiter interrupted.

"Are we?" Bambi posed the question to her roommate.

"I think I would prefer the salmon," Anna May said.

"You're reading my mind," Bambi said. She turned to the waiter. "We'll both have the Salmon à la Vierge, and two more glasses of wine." He bowed and retired to the kitchen to place the order.

"Are you feeling okay?"

"Yeah, I'm fine." Anna May looked like she wanted to say something.

"What is it, darling? Something is eatin' at you...I know."

Anna May squirmed in her chair before she spoke. "Look, Bambi. I really appreciate everything you and the company are doing for me, but I'm not sure I can live up to all this."

"I don't understand." Bambi furrowed her brow.

"Neither do I, and that's the problem. You're being very kind, and I want you to know that I appreciate it." She paused. "Please don't take me wrong. You're the sweetest person I've ever met, but why all this attention? Why are you guys going to so much trouble? I'm just a nobody who happened to read her grandmother's notes and connected a few dots. I'm by no means as special as everyone's making me out to be. You don't need a masters to see that."

Bambi took on a serious expression. "Look, baby-doll. I'm gonna level with you, okay?"

Anna May nodded.

"I want you to know I like you very much...and I apologize if I come across as pushy." She was obviously choosing her words carefully. "To be totally honest, I've been instructed not to let you out of my sight."

"But...why?"

"They don't tell me why. They just say, Bambi, you do this or Bambi, you do that and I have to do what they say."

"Am I in danger, Bambi?" Anna May had an alarmed expression on her face.

Bambi moved in closer and lowered her voice. "You asked me that once before and I gave you a really stupid answer. I apologize for that. But I might as well fess up." She whispered, "Someone has been following you ever since you set foot in D.C. I'm surprised the FBI didn't catch on the minute ya'll got off the plane."

"You were there? I mean...at the airport when I got here?"

"Yes."

"Well...who is it?"

"It's not an 'it'...it's more like a 'them'. Again, I'm being honest. We don't know the why. I was sent out on a routine surveillance mission. It's standard procedure when a VIP visits the company. It really is S.O.P. We want to know if a visitor is being followed. Mostly, it turns out to be a waste of time. But, believe me, dearie, somebody is *very* interested in you, and we haven't concluded as to who, what or why."

"You're not just a secretary, are you, Bambi?"

Bambi stared into Anna May's eyes. "I can't answer that. Not right now. As far as you're concerned, at the moment, that's all I am."

"Are they using me as bait?"

"Absolutely not...don't you ever get that idea. I'll just say this. There are sharks in the water, honey. You're on somebody's radar. Anyway, it's best we don't talk about these things in public. There's plenty of time for that later. Right now, just you remember three things: One, you are being followed and two, you are among friends, and three, you *will* be protected."

Chapter Twelve
Chung-hee Graduates

B y the sixth week of his eight-week training course, Chung-hee was formally accepted as an honorary 'White Tiger', a name given to a soldier in the 707th Special Mission Battalion, and he was allowed to wear the official White Tiger emblem on his battle fatigues.

In addition to skills in the martial arts, he had become proficient in the use of the H&K MP5 sub-machine gun, the Benelli Tactical Super-90 shotgun, and a host of other high-tech weaponry.

He had acquired another ten pounds of solid muscle, lost any shyness he may have had, and was quickly becoming one *bad-ass* killing machine.

From day one he had been taught the importance of *teamwork* — taking the focus from himself and redirecting it to the group.

The beginning of the seventh week of his indoctrination, training began to diverge along lines that were mission specific. The exercises were grueling and went on around the clock with little more than four hours of sleep in a single, twenty-four-hour period. Rewards, when given, consisted of things like, being able to stand by a fire and rest, or to sit or sleep for a few minutes. Food was essential, and the group received four hot meals a day, sometimes falling asleep while they ate.

Chung-hee was determined not to be the weakest link in the group, but his lack of experience often showed through his determination to succeed. It was during those times that he developed complete respect for his team members. They were the ones that brought him through, and it was made clear to him that no man begrudged him for his lack of abilities. To the man, any one of them was eager to carry him, if necessary, through the successful completion of a task. His cockiness soon evolved into a sense of appreciation and only caused him to try harder.

Each successful completion of an exercise was followed by a resounding 'Hoo-rah', the battle cry of the battalion.

* * *

First Lieutenant Marshall Lewis, a black officer in his twenties, wheeled a cart into Anna May's office at 3:45 PM and helped her arrange the folders in her filing cabinet.

Each folder was sealed and marked '*** TOP SECRET ***'. Marshall broke the seal on the first folder and showed Anna May how to sign her name to the list of names that preceded her. Then he instructed her as to how to open a directory on her desktop, where a catalogue of each folder was kept.

All the folders she had in her possession appeared on the list. When she opened one, she was to open the subdirectory of the numbered folder and select from a choice of radio buttons— 'Sealed in safe', 'Open in safe', 'In use', 'Closed in safe', and 'Done'.

When reading she was to select 'In Use', when not reading, she would return the folder to the filing cabinet and select 'Closed in safe'.

When the cabinet was closed, it would lock automatically. If the cabinet was left open for longer than three minutes, security would appear to check on it. When she had finished with a folder, she would select 'Done' and Lieutenant Lewis would come and pick it up.

He told her the folders were not to be taken from her office, when viewing them she was to keep her door locked at all times and no one was allowed to see the contents unless they wore a *** TOP SECRET *** badge, and they were required to sign on a flysheet attached to the folder indicating they had been given access to the contents. He gave her a form to sign accepting receipt of the folders and declaring she had read and understood all the rules and regulations regarding this specific set of documents. He left her office at 4:15.

She opened the file marked 'Peter Langstrum—November 1, 1965—November 30, 1965', since this was the period that most interested her at the moment.

Scanning down to November 17th, she found notes regarding a meeting with Dr. Harry Robinson.

Langstrum's notes revealed Robinson's theory, that at some point during the Paleozoic period, between 530 to 540 million years ago, there was a single event that kick-started the process of evolution.

Fossil records showed untold millions of new creatures from unknown origins appearing in a very short time, and these new organisms created multiple trees of life—not just the single tree as explained by Darwin. He further theorized, since the time of the Cambrian Explosion, evolution had slowed down. He believed the answer to his theory could be found in the evolution machinery of DNA. Further, he believed altering evolutionary machinery of a single DNA molecule might result in the onset of an entirely new Cambrian Explosion—

"My God," she murmured. "Robinson wasn't afraid they might stop evolution, he was afraid they might inadvertently spur a new event, such as the one occurring over 530 million years ago, causing evolution to suddenly crank up and spin out of control."

The theory of evolution suggested evolution had been a slow, methodical journey of 'trial and error'. Mistakes were corrected through the process of 'natural selection', eliminating undesirable mutations before they had time to replicate. If left alone, the process of evolution had proven to be a remarkably simple system of creating order out of chaos. But if tampered with? The idea of the sudden appearance of billions of new organisms competing with humanity was chilling.

She leaned back in her chair and rubbed her eyes, thinking of the possibilities. *The sudden reappearance of the dinosaurs—or worse.*

* * *

Kim Bong Hwa had stumbled upon research materials written by Russian micro-biologists suggesting human DNA consisted of ten percent effectual DNA and ninety-percent junk. He believed junk DNA could record and retain new information that could subsequently be passed on to a subject's offspring. The influences of affirmations had long been known to affect human behavior, and that behavior was passed down through generations.

He also believed DNA could be affected through the use of *endogenous DNA laser radiation*; by modulating certain frequency patterns onto a laser-like ray, then exposing DNA to the ray, influencing DNA frequency and modifying DNA genetic information.

To the Pakistani, the first evidence of change was internal. He became acutely aware of sounds that would normally be of no particular interest. He began to feel colors. Desperation, a feeling he had felt since his capture, was waning. He began to sleep less, and he often awoke at odd times. Also, his powers of concentration had sharpened.

Kim Bong Hwa noticed a roughness to Hussein's skin and the slightest horizontal elongation of his pupils. He wondered if his patient was developing the means of steering the process himself... a possibility that had just recently entered his mind. Certain events had occurred that made the scientist wonder if Hussein was developing hyper-communications, and at times he sensed he was the one being studied.

The Pakistani had stopped talking completely, not that anything he had said previously provided Kim Bong Hwa with any useful information. He always seemed to be focused on one thing at a time. Once the scientist thought he saw something move on his desk...for no apparent reason. On impulse, he switched his gaze to the Pakistani. He caught him staring at that very spot.

* * *

At 7:00 p.m. there was a knock on the door and Anna May opened it to come face to face with Tom Martin.

"You must be Anna May Lee," the young man said.

"You're Tom," she answered.

"In the flesh...May I come in?"

Anna May realized she was gawking at him and suddenly felt self-conscience.

"Oh, I'm sorry, Tom. I don't know what I was thinking. Yes, of course, please come in."

"I have that effect on women." He smiled.

"Bambi will be ready in a minute," she said, backing away to make room for him to enter.

"Aren't you coming with us?" he asked as he seated himself on the couch.

"I don't think so, Tom. Not tonight. I have a lot of work to catch up on and Bob is coming in tomorrow night. Can I get you something?"

"No thanks. How are you getting on in your new job?"

"Can we talk about something else?" she said. "I'm new, and I'm really not supposed to discuss my work away from the agency."

"It's strange, isn't it?"

"Strange?"

"Yeah, I remember when I got my clearance, I was afraid to talk to anybody about anything. It takes some time to get used to it. It's good you're being cautious.

"Say, to change the subject, have you ever been to Louisiana?"

"No, but I hear it's beautiful there."

"Bambi and I are planning to fly down weekend after next. I'm going to take her deep-sea fishing. Maybe you and Bob would like to come along?"

"I'll have to discuss it with Bob, but I think I would like that very much."

"Bob's with the FBI, right?"

"Yes, he works in the office with computers."

"Really?"

"He cracks systems the bureau confiscates—mostly tax evasion cases."

"That must be interesting."

"I think he'd rather be in the field where the action is."

"I'm cooped up in the office most of the time myself. I know how he must feel, especially in L.A. where the weather's always so nice."

"You two getting acquainted?" Bambi said as she entered the room.

"You look stunning," Tom said, getting up from the couch.

"You sure you'll be okay here?" Bambi said to Anna May.

"I've got plenty to keep me busy."

"Well, don't work too hard."

"I won't. I'll work for about an hour and get to bed early. I've got a big day ahead of me tomorrow."

Anna May told Tom how nice it was to meet him and the happy couple left for a night on the town.

Later that evening, Anna May booted up her laptop and began looking for an apartment in the D.C. area. The choices appeared to be limitless. Planning on keeping their apartment in L.A. she had to be concerned with their budget. About 2:00 a.m. she awoke to hear Bambi and Tom return from their outing. The sound of their muffled voices stopped with the closing of Bambi's bedroom door. She wished Bob was there lying beside her.

She didn't go back to sleep directly. She began to think about the theory of evolution as put forth by Charles Darwin. How he claimed that all life forms evolved from microscopic single cell organisms. Where they came from, no one was sure. Scientific theories are just that—theories that have yet to be proven.

The Cambrian Explosion referred to a brief period of

earth's existence where around forty-one new paths, call phyla, had evolved quite suddenly, expressed as happening within one minute of a twenty-four-hour day. Only *that* one-minute may have lasted for twenty to thirty-million years.

Darwin's theory of evolution tried to prove that life evolved without the hand of a grand designer. While it is easy to accept subtle changes, such as the changes in the beaks of birds and the spots on the wings of moths, when geneticists considered the evolution of a complex organ such as the human eye, which was also believed to have appeared during the same twenty to thirty-million year-span of time, logic gets thrown out of the window.

If insects that are red in color are eaten less than insects that are brown, you end up with fewer brown insects and more red ones. This was called the theory of natural selection. But how did the different colored insects come to be in the first place?

What natural selection process could cause a human eye to evolve unless...the instructions for the alteration in the human eye were already present in the DNA before something or *someone* turned on the switch that started the processes?

The only reasonable explanation was akin to a computer program that had built in it a subroutine that only kicked into action after a certain set of events were satisfied—like a burglar alarm that switches on when someone opens a door. Otherwise, the subroutine that controlled the alarm might have never occurred at all. How many other subroutines are hidden inside a person's DNA that have yet to be executed? It's what we don't know that holds the greatest mysteries of all. And to cap it all off, why would an intelligence create a particular set of events unless they were expected to occur?

The fact that human evolution appears to have slowed down did not mean that evolution itself was coming to an end. It's possible that thousands, even millions of pre-programmed subroutines in DNA were waiting their turn to be switched on, or off. After all, the switches that controlled evolution had already be documented by Floyd Romesberg...

The alarm sounded at 6:15 a.m..

* * *

During the last two weeks of Chung-hee's training, his team performed exercises with the U.S. Army's Delta Force under the command of Colonel Michael Hager. On the final day, he was ready for deployment behind North Korean lines. He wasn't the least bit concerned.

Chapter Thirteen
Abduction

Anna May stared at her computer screen. It was filled with nonsensical formulas and esoteric algorithms that defied her imagination.

This guy is all over the place, she thought. She began to question Kim Bong Hwa's sanity. He had started so many unfinished projects that she found it difficult to figure out where he was going with his research.

Frustrated, she embarked on a binary search exercise in which she started in the middle of the documents and split them by date until she found something that made sense. Then she would backtrack, halfway between that point and the previous position, and continue from there.

About two-thirds into the stack, she found what she was looking for. Kim Bong Hwa had a subject, an American of Pakistani descent. She picked up the phone and pressed MISC. Sally Gooden answered.

"Hi, Sally. It's Anna May Lee."

"Oh...hi, Ms. Lee. Do you need something?"

"Can you find out if an American citizen has been reported missing from South Korea...within the past six months?"

"Oh, golly, sure. Do you have a name?"

"I'm afraid not, dear, but he, or his parents may have been born in Pakistan. It's just a hunch."

"Okay, I'll get right on it, Ms. Lee. I'll call you back when I find something."

Ten minutes later, Anna May's phone rang.

"Hi, Ms. Lee. It's Sally Gooden."

"Uh, huh."

"Six months ago, a man matching that general description left the Gongneung branch of the Professor Wolf's English Academy on a trip north. He was an instructor of Intermediate Business English, and at least one of his students had a suspicion he was going to try to get a meeting with Kim Jong-un. They say he was upset about human rights violations. He hasn't been heard from since."

"Did you get a name?"

"Sure did. His name is Hussein Mehraj Khan and he's about twenty-eight, dark hair, brown eyes and he wears glasses."

"Did anyone know where he was originally from?"

"His work application says he graduated from Boston University. He has a master's degree in Political Science."

"Political science—and he was teaching English?"

"Pardon?"

"I was just thinking out loud, Sally. Thanks, you've been a tremendous help."

"My pleasure, Ms. Lee. Anytime... Say, do you want his Boston address?"

"Go ahead and give it to me."

"927 North Victor Circle, Apartment 27C in Cambridge."

"Thanks, Sally."

Anna May wrote a memo to Major Atkins and continued with her research.

Biologists generally agreed, evolution takes place over millennia, but ecological change can occur much faster—sometimes in a matter of days. A recent study by Cornell suggested evolution and ecology can operate in the same time scale.

The field of *Evolutionary Ecology* had remained a much-neglected field, as evolution researchers were concerned more with the pattern of evolution and its genetic and developmental correlates than with the ecological causes of evolution, while ecologists often ignored the evolutionary implications of population and community processes.

Genetic switches allowed and organism to modulate its phenotype in response to environmental changes. Kim Bong Hwa appeared to be attempting to do the same thing with gene modification.

Bob's plane arrived on time at Dulles International, and Anna May met him in the baggage area. Bambi and Tom loaded his luggage into Tom's Mercedes and offered to take the couple for a drink. They hit it off famously and didn't get back to the apartment until 1:00 a.m..

Bob and Tom talked on and on about deep-sea fishing in the Gulf of Mexico. Tom had his boat docked at Shell Beach south of New Orleans and had the group rolling in laughter about some of his most memorable fishing trips.

Saturday morning, Anna May showed Bob the list of apartments she liked. Bambi loaned them her car, and the two went out on the hunt.

They settled on a furnished townhome at the Avalon Crescent apartment complex with two bedrooms and two baths, a nice walk-in closet and a cozy kitchen. The rent was within their budget, and the grounds were beautiful. It was close to the CIA offices and had nice shopping areas nearby. They signed the lease and put up the deposit. They agreed with the manager to move in on Tuesday.

* * *

Five blades of an MH-X Advanced Special Operations Helicopter, each spanning some seven meters, spun silently through the darkness at tree-top level as it passed over the North Korean border. Chung-hee, Dong-sun and three South Korean Special Forces soldiers sat inside. The air was cool. Except for the faint glow of LEDs along the floor, the journey was made in total darkness. The only indication of movement was a slight vibration on the deck. The mixture of smells from the jungle below brought back memories of Chung-hee's trek through the jungles to make his escape — to where he did not know. It seemed like only yesterday he was being tortured to the brink of insanity.

Now, he was going back. Gone was the fear that had controlled his actions since as long as he could remember. As a phoenix rising from the ashes, he had reassembled his body parts into a formidable weapon, and he was straining at the leash to put them into action, which didn't go unnoticed by Dong-sun and the rest of the crew. Like a guided missile, his thoughts were of neither life nor death——only on the target and the success of the mission.

* * *

Two weeks had passed since Bob gained access to the North Korean mainframe. Through a stroke of genius, he had circumvented the link provided by *the company* and created a virtual network of his own design. He made it so he could access it from home.

Anna May had accompanied Bambi to the weekly female gathering at the Congressional Bar & Grill, and Bob chewed on a slab of reheated pizza from the refrigerator and drank from a half-empty bottle of Chardonnay. That's when he found it, a second link between the CIA and the North Korean Cray XT5 Jaguar supercomputer.

He needed to obtain the root account password which guarded the entrance to the partition holding the data. It was not likely the password had been poorly chosen or fit some predictable characteristics. He was fortunate to be able to use the computing power of the Cray to run his code-cracking software. He was not surprised to learn, without the benefit of proper support, the Koreans had left a *QUSER* account available to take him into a general area where he could insert his code. Only 17% of the CPU was being used. The amount available for the cracker software to be implanted was way in excess of what was needed to do the job.

After he gained entrance to the root directory, he was able to examine the ports without being detected. He was surprised to find an open port showing traffic through a server located in San Francisco. In a separate window, he logged into the data center at the CIA, and through a process of elimination, he found a data stream which directly coincided with the data coming from the Cray in North Korea. *Are they spying on us or are we spying on them?* he wondered. It was not the virtual link he already had access to.

* * *

Anna May and Bambi exited the bar at 11:00 PM and walked the half-block to where Bambi's car had been parked. A derelict approached Bambi demanding money, causing her to not take notice of the short Asian man approaching from the opposite direction. The Asian jammed a gun into Bambi's back. She spun around and knocked the weapon from his hand. The derelict produced an instrument of some kind and slammed it down on the back of Bambi's head, sending her sprawling to the pavement.

The pain shot through her head like a hot knife. As she struggled to get to her feet, she saw the Asian man force Anna May into the side of a van and watched it as it careened around the corner. Her purse was nowhere in sight. *No purse, no keys, no cell phone. Dammit. How could I be so stupid?*

She attempted to flag down a passing car. The car swerved to avoid her and kept on going. 'SHIT," she screamed. She didn't have the time to ask permission.

The next car found Bambi standing in the middle of the road with a Colt 45 pistol she had produced from a leg holster underneath her skirt. She aimed it directly at the driver. The car came to a complete stop. The driver was staring back at her like a hypnotized deer.

Bambi moved to the driver's door. She pulled an official looking badge out of her blouse.

"Get out," she said. "I need your car."

The man fumbled for the door handle and Bambi pulled on it so hard, he poured out into the street, eyes wild with fright.

"Do you have a cell phone?" she said.

The driver, now standing in a pool of his own urine, shook his head.

"Get to a phone. Call this number at CIA headquarters at

Langley, she handed him her card. Ask for the EAL. You got that? The EAL."

The man acknowledged by nodding his head. Sweat rolled down his forehead and ran off the end of his nose.

"Tell them Agent Marshall has taken your car." She paused. "Do you know your own license number?"

With both his eyes and his mouth wide open, he nodded again.

"Give them your license number, and a description of your car. You got that?"

"Yes, m..ma'am."

* * *

Anna May sat in the back of the van. The men hadn't attempted to tie her up. *They are in one hell of a hurry to get somewhere*, she thought. As they passed Westover Village, she slipped her hand in her skirt pocket, felt along the face of her Blackberry and held down the '9' key. The men were arguing in a language she didn't understand. She covered the speaker with the palm of her hand and prayed the 911 operator would not hang up.

* * *

After a few minutes of frantic searching, Bambi realized she would never find the van on her own. She swerved into a convenience store and called Bob.

"Anna May?" he blurted out.

"No, it's Bambi," she answered. "Two guys took her."

"I know, they're headed to Dulles."

"How do you know that?"

"It's hard to explain. I believe they've got a late flight booked on Air China to Beijing."

"Call the agency... No, don't," she corrected herself. "Meet me there. Do you know how to get to Dulles?"

"I think so."

"It's out 267 west. You can't miss it."

"Okay. I'm on my way."

Bob dashed to his rental car, got behind the driver's seat, and sped away.

Bambi pressed the accelerator down hard. As she crossed the 465 Loop, she looked down at the speedometer. She was doing 115 MPH. It didn't take long before she had company. "Oh great," she said to herself. She touched her brakes, but the cruiser pulled up alongside. The officer signaled for her to roll down here window. Then he mouthed the words, "Where are we going?"

God! That's a relief, she thought.

She mouthed back the word "Dulles". The cop soon had his cruiser up to 120 MPH. Bambi held tight to his rear bumper like Tony Stewart at Daytona. They weaved in and out of traffic...one cruiser in front and two behind.

Bob was stopped in Arlington. He presented his FBI identification and the officer let him go. He thought about explaining the situation to the cop, but he had lost too much time already.

Bambi rushed through the front door of Dulles International Airport with three of Washington D.C.'s finest. People scampered out of their way as the entourage raced through the concourse. They sailed through the security checkpoint with all alarms sounding. Soon, they were joined by three federal security guards. When they arrived at the far end of the concourse, it was empty. The gate was closed and the DC-10 was already on the taxiway.

Bambi produced her badge and waved it at a group of star-tled gate attendants. "Stop the plane," she demanded. "Stop the goddamned plane." They simply stared at her like she was some crazy woman having a nervous breakdown over missing her flight. One flight attendant was busy punching numbers on her phone like she was trying to kill it.

As security guards chattered over their radios, Bambi raced through the jet bridge and flew down the steel stairway leading to the ground. She left one broken high-heel shoe on the steps and kicked off the other shoe as she dashed to a nearby fuel truck, jumping in next to a startled driver with half a po-boy sandwich jammed in his jaws.

Showing her badge, and her gun, she shouted, "We've got to stop that Air China DC-10. Get this crate out there and put yourself between it and the air."

"But lady..."

She flashed her badge. "Get your ass in gear, mister. We don't have time to get acquainted."

Without another word, the driver started the bob-tail truck and sped off down the taxiway. The DC-10 was sitting at the end of the runway, making its final turn.

"Faster, goddamnit," she shouted.

"Geeezus, lady! I'm going as fast as I can," the driver shouted.

"Turn left," she demanded.

"But, lady, there's no concrete there."

"*Turn,* I said," she demanded as she pointed her Colt directly at his head. "Get out in front of that damned plane or kill us both trying."

The man drove off the concrete taxiway and onto the grass. Dirt flew from the wheels of the truck as the heavy fuel carrier bounced over the uneven ground. The thundering roar of the

DC-10's powerful engines made further conversation impossible. It was accelerating its engines for the takeoff.

"Faster, damnit," she screamed over the howl of the jet's engines.

The driver didn't acknowledge. Deafness had overtaken him. His knuckles were white on the wheel and he gritted his teeth as they sailed over a drainage ditch.

Bouncing up on top of the tarmac as the plane started to roll, the driver made a sudden stop. Bambi jumped from the passenger seat, positioned herself in front of the truck, spread her legs in a defiant stance, grabbed her pistol with both hands, and aimed it directly at the pilot in the cockpit.

* * *

"What the f..." the pilot said as he threw a glance at his co-pilot.

His partner, jabbering in Cantonese, threw up his hands, expecting a shower of broken glass. The engineer dived for the deck.

An instant later, the pilot cut back on the throttle, jammed his foot on the brakes and the DC-10 sat idling at the start of the runway as police vehicles came rolling in from every direction.

Chapter Fourteen
On North Korean Soil

The chopper gently set down in a small clearing in a dense forest on a mountain about four miles north-northwest of their objective. From where they stood, there were no heat signatures for a mile in all directions. The camp itself was surrounded by mountains.

In-su exited first, followed by Jin-sang, Kwang-ho, Chung-hee and Dong-sun. With a sign of 'thumbs-up' from Dong-sun, the chopper lifted quietly into the darkness. Dong-sun read their coordinates as North 42 degrees, 35 minutes, 31.73 seconds, and East 129 degrees, 52 minutes, 36.66 seconds, at an altitude of 1,883 feet above sea-level.

His plan was to follow a logging road southwest, then follow a path that made a gentle descent four-hundred feet down the side of the mountain to intersect with the railroad tracks on the north side of the camp's fence and then ride on the rods under the train until it passed through the camp's gate and stopped. There would be only one stationary guard as the train arrived late at night.

Recent satellite images had been consistent. The train

always pulled exactly 15 rail cars and stopped at the same point inside the camp every time, with the preferred point of debarkation being at the tenth and eleventh rail car.

The train always arrived after midnight on Wednesdays and was unloaded the next morning by the prisoners inside the camp. This train never carried passengers, only provisions such as food, clothing and medical supplies. One last check of their equipment and the team began making their way toward the logging road.

In-su took the point. He was the most experienced of the group and the one who had seen the most action. Recently, he had returned from a combat mission with the US Marines in Afghanistan. For his actions there, he had been awarded the Silver Star for valor in the face of the enemy—and honor never before bestowed upon a soldier of the South Korean Republic of Korea Armed Forces.

Jin-sang was the quiet one. He was unusually tall by Korean standards and Chung-hee had stuck him with the nickname of 'Michael Jordan', an American basketball star. In the last days of their training, the team had watched their first American basketball game. When Jordan was presented with a lifetime achievement award during the half-time show, Chung-hee pointed at Jin-sang and shouted 'Michael Jordan'. Jin-sang hung his head and the other men laughed.

Kwang-ho was the runt. Barely 5'-1" in stature, he was the fastest runner in the team. No one could pass Kwang-ho on the track. If he sensed a runner breathing down his neck, he would unleash an amazing spurt of energy that was simply remarkable.

After Jin-sang received the moniker of *Michael Jordan*, Colonel Hager decided Kwang-ho's name should be *Man-of-War*, after a famous American racehorse. When the meaning was explained to Kwang-ho, Kwang-ho accepted the title with pride.

After that, everybody got an American nickname. Chung-hee was called *Little Boy* after the second atomic bomb dropped on Japan in WWII, and Dong-sun was called a Korean word that loosely translated to 'Old Hardass'. He gladly accepted his nickname as the others had accepted theirs.

The forest around them was deathly quiet. The team leader, Dong-sun, consulted his GPS and mapped out the best course to intercept the railroad tracks that led into the camp. The latest satellite images estimated the train would arrive at the camp at 47 minutes after midnight. According to Chung-hee, the train slowed down to a crawl 100 meters before it entered Camp 22, and that's where they would crawl under the train and ride on the rods into the camp. They had three hours to make the four-mile hike. With the surrounding terrain, and some areas appearing more challenging than others, they had little time to lose.

High-resolution images from a geostationary orbital satellite, processed and combined with a topographical map using powerful mainframe computers at the National Geospatial Intelligence Agency, began appearing on the screens of their GPS units. Even in darkness, objects as small as six-inches in diameter were easily discernable.

* * *

Kim Bong Hwa peered into the cage of his 'experiment' who was asleep on the bunk. The Pakistani-American had been transformed into a hideous monster that bared little resemblance to his former self. This was not what Kim Bong Hwa had expected. Although the creature appeared to remain docile, the scientist went back to locking him in his cage at night. He shuddered to imagine what changes the next twenty-four-hours might bring.

Had his prisoner lost the defiance he exhibited by not reacting aggressively to the torture he received prior to being taken to the scientist, or was he just dying like all the rest? The scientists wondered.

Immediately after supper, Kim Bong Hwa had been summoned to attend the night's entertainment, the execution of another family in the glass gas chamber. He didn't particularly want to go. He went only because it was expected of him. Watching four more of the thousands of inmates being continuously exterminated was hardly his idea of after-dinner entertainment, but if he didn't appear and take notes, it would be viewed as a slight against the party, and no one wanted to be added to that list.

The chamber was sealed air-tight, 3.5 meters wide, 3 meters long, and 2.2 meters high. There was an injection tube entering the unit to deliver the lethal dose of poison. Families usually stuck together and individuals without families would normally cower in the corners. Scientists sat above them and took copious notes.

This event was no different from the others he had attended —parents vomiting and choking while attempting to give mouth-to-mouth recitation to their dying children.

Kim Bong Hwa felt no sympathy or pity for these *criminals* that he was certain were responsible for the horrific conditions in his country, and he had begun to see these executions as a waste of his valuable time.

He was certain he could find a more efficient solution, not only for the inmates of Camp 22, but for all the enemies of the DPRK inside and outside his beloved country. It was disgusting to be sure, so to pass the time, he concentrated on thinking of his new assistant who was due to arrive at any moment. *Maybe she would be able to provide the key he needed to give him the answer he had been searching for.*

When he learned of the existence of Diane Walter's granddaughter, the wheels of his depraved brain began to spin. When he discovered the girl would shortly be awarded a PhD in molecular biology, he nearly peed in his pants. It was a great stroke of luck that his American informer had finally come across with something that would be worth the money he had deposited in a Swiss bank account. On arrival, if she refused to cooperate, he would lock her in the cage with his monster for a time. If the thought of a similar fate didn't produce the desired results, he would think of something else.

All that changed when he finally had the time to check his e-mail. It was a great disappointment to receive news of the failed abduction of Anna May Lee, one that would cause him no small amount of despair. The only bright spot was the news that the kidnapper had managed to commit suicide after the botched kidnap attempt.

* * *

A light snow covered the ground as the team approached the point where they would make their way down the slope to the bottom of the mountain. They moved cautiously, stopping to check for heat signatures in the immediate area. The air was crisp and cold. "Are you okay?" Dong-sun asked Chung-hee.

Chung-hee merely grinned and whispered, "Hoo-rah," as they continued down the incline.

Reaching the area where they would wait for the train, the team stopped. The locomotive's whistle could be heard coming from the southeast. The train showed up as a bright green image on the GPS device. As it came into sight, it cast a bright light along the tracks from its one, huge cyclops pointed in their direction. They would have to take cover and wait until the engine passed before they would make a mad dash to roll under the train and climb up onto the rods.

The plan had been meticulously engineered by the CIA. Four members of the team were to enter the camp hidden under the 10th and 11th rail car... Two men under each car. Dong-sun with Chung-hee under the 10th car, and In-su with Jin-sang under the one directly behind it. Kwang-ho would remain behind hidden in the rocks and stay in constant contact with the other members of the team. The mission was to capture or kill, if necessary, Kim Bong Hwa, collect any physical data and disable the Cray computer, and get back to Kwang-ho without being detected.

Dong-sun carried a thumb drive that contained the software that would be inserted into the computer's operating system that would instantly close all incoming and outgoing ports to prevent it from being shut down until the job was finished... about one minute. After that, the entire system would take on the capabilities of a brick.

The loose cannon on the operation was Chung-hee. Everyone knew that. His job was to point the way to the scientist's lair and get his three partners in and out of the camp without being detected. After living in the camp since his birth until the time he had escaped, he was certain there was only one building in the camp that could house a computer and offices.

Psychologists were divided on how Chung-hee might react when confronted with his past. Especially if encountering a camp guard. But in the end, they resigned themselves to Dong-sun's advice that he knew his men and he would never allow

Chung-hee to go on the mission if he had any concerns as to Chung-hee's loyalty or his ability to make the mission a success.

In secret, Dong-sun still held some concern as to the ramifications of Chung-hee's actions if confronted with his tormentors and had instructed the other team members to kill Chung-hee if he should jeopardize the mission. If Chung-hee were killed, Dong-sun's orders were to strip him of his clothes and leave him in the compound. The North Koreans might be curious as to how he got back into the camp, but it was doubtful they would be able to prove the Americans were involved in a raid.

No recent intel on the Pakistani-American was available, but they were forced to assume they would not encounter him during the operation.

The entire exercise was to look like an inside job. If any of the team members should be captured, they were instructed to use the 'rapid-death' pills that were issued. They were to carry no identification, and no one entertained the idea of being tortured to death in a North Korean prison camp.

The only planned death was that of the lone guard at the gate who would receive a poison administered by a 'heart attack gun'. They were taking a big chance by risking an international incident if the Chinese became involved.

As the train came closer to the camp, it began to decelerate. The blue and white Chinese locomotive approached the team's position at a snail's space. The soft roar of the DFH-3's diesel engines came first, followed by the clacking of the wheels of the fifteen green and yellow rail cars that followed and coming to a complete stop just a few feet from the gate.

From inside the camp, a guard opened one side of the gate, secured it, and then did the same to the other side. A second camp guard, only there temporarily, approached the train, climbed aboard, and spoke with the engineer, as the first guard shined a light down both sides of the cars attached. The second guard exited the train and went back into the camp in the darkness, most likely to call it a day and get some rest.

The first guard flagged the locomotive through the gate. The Janney couplers banged one at a time from the front of the train to the last car in the line. This was the team's cue to begin scrambling to the undersides of the cars with the sound of couplers masking their activity.

Since they would only travel a short distance, the four team members had no trouble holding on to the rods that ran through the center beams underneath the rail cars until they reached their planned destinations, hidden from view by anyone in the camp. The first guard closed and locked the gate and went back into the guardhouse.

Chung-hee, would then guide them to where he was certain the scientist's lab was located. It was not deep underground as Kim Bong Hwa had described it to his Pakistani-American guest but located in the administrative building near the spot where they had disembarked from the rail cars. Inch by inch they made their way toward their intended destination.

* * *

After a night's rest, Anna May was released from Walter-Reed National Military Medical Center and accompanied by Bob her fiancée, Capt. Bambi Marshall, and a Secret Service detail to the George Bush Center, the headquarters of the Central Intelligence Agency for a debriefing.

"Bambi, all this time I thought you were a secretary," Anna May spoke. "Turns out you're some kind of super cop that stared down a DC-10 in your *stocking feet* just to save little old me."

"I hope you're not mad at me," Bambi replied.

"Don't be silly, Bambi. If it hadn't been for you, I'd probably be dead by now, because they would never have gotten this girl to talk.

"What kind of drug did they give me, anyway?"

"Nothing complicated, I assure you. The toxicologist described it as a common date-rape drug that wore off after a few hours. Apparently, they had instructions to be sure you arrived at your destination in good condition.

"We had to let the plane go, the guy sitting with you flashed his diplomatic immunity papers and we had no other choice. Someone at the Chinese embassy tried to raise a stink about it, but nothing will come of it. You were obviously an American citizen being taken against your will, and they'd rather it be forgotten.

"I should have been more careful, Anna May. That guy came out of nowhere and the other guy blindsided me before I could reach my pistol."

"Bambi, stop it. You did your best, and it's all anyone could expect you to do. I've been thinking about why they wanted me in the first place, and I think Bong Hwa is stumped and he thinks I can help him solve his problem."

Chapter Fifteen
Inside The Camp

C hung-hee was right when he said most of the guards would be sleeping when they arrived at the camp. The team wore military-style ballistic vests, military ski masks, were equipped with a highly secret *heart attack gun* created by the CIA in the 1970s, 9-millimeter Glocks fitted with silencers, and Garrote wire to strangle the victim if you could get close enough behind without being detected. The main objective was to kidnap the doctor and get out without being seen. To maintain secrecy, only one death had been planned.

The murder weapon was the *heart attack gun*, practically silent, it penetrated the victim's clothing and left only a tiny red dot where the poison entered the body. Only a skilled pathologist who knew what to look for would ever discover the victim's heart attack wasn't from natural causes.

Chung-hee and Dong-sun took the lead and In-su and Jin-sang followed close behind.

As the two teams crept along the walls of the buildings used for storing supplies, they were somewhat surprised at the complete lack of activity in their general area, then they began to see why. The administrative section of the camp was isolated from the rest of the camp by a twelve-foot-high electrified fence which was closed at night to prevent prisoners from wandering into the administrative area or to the main gate. There were no guards present because no one was supposed to be in the administrative area after dark. The teams were able to make their way into the administration building unobserved. Now they had their first problem, *Where in the Hell was Bong Hwa?*

They decided to wait for five minutes and listen for a sound for any indication that someone other than themselves was in the building, and there they remained until they heard a human voice cursing in *Cháoxiǎnyǔ*. Kim Bong Hwa was cursing in the language of North Korea about his watch. The team slowly advanced toward the sound of Bong Hwa's voice and saw a door midway down a corridor toward the East that cast a light under the door that spilled out into the hall. Approaching the room they observed a shadow under the door that indicated activity from inside the room.

Bong Hwa seemed to be talking to someone, but they only heard Bong Hwa's side of the conversation. After a minute or so more, they came to the conclusion that Bong Hwa was carrying on a conversation with someone that was not talking back.

Dong-sun whispered that the other person was probably deceased and Bong Hwa was addressing him, or her, without the expectation of receiving a reply.

The next thing that occurred happened too fast for the scientist to even utter a grunt. The team had taped his mouth, put a bag over his head and set him down on the floor with a soft thud that shook his spine like he had been kicked in the rear end by a mule. He tried to complain, but Dong-sun said something in his native language that caused him to go mute.

They observed the person that lay on a cot in a cage who

was obviously dead and literally melting. Jan-sang found the keys to the cage and managed to get blood and tissue samples and placed them into a plastic bag.

Checking to eliminate any sign that they had been there, the men, with Chung-hee in tow, made their way to the entrance and out of the building. Then to the train where Dong-sun disappeared under one of the cars near the end of the train and merged on the other side.

Slowly, he made his way to the lone guard's station where the guard was seated and snoring loudly. He then positioned the heart attack gun near the main artery in the guard's neck and pressed the trigger. Almost instantly, the guard fell forward and was stopped by the shelf where a pornographic book he had been reading lay open and turned on its pages to save his place.

The rest of the team and Bong Hwa emerged from the rear of the train, Dong-sun threw them the keys to the gate, and they opened it wide enough to escape and tossed the keys back to Dong-sun who placed them next to the book on the shelf in the guard hut, slipped out through the gate, relocked the gate from the outside and together they made their way to Kwang-ho, making sure the area held no evidence of their being there and made their way up the mountain and back to where the chopper would be waiting. Altogether a flawless operation.

Chung-hee received a great deal of attention on the way back to the chopper. It was then that he realized he had passed an important test and had at last been accepted as a true brother and permanent member of the South Korean Army. South Korea was his home now, and he felt tremendous pride in that.

Chapter Sixteen
Final Meeting at Langley

Anna May Lee took her seat in the main conference room of CIA headquarters at Langley. Anna May recognized some of the attendees from when she was in the same room before, but there were several new men and women that were not introduced.

"Ms. Lee," the Chairman began, have you come to any conclusions about the DPRK's involvement in *The Ladder Project*?

"I believe I have, Mr. Chairman," Anna May replied.

"Then let's hear it."

"When *The Ladder Project* began in 1967, the original purpose of the project was to create a simple life form that could survive on the moon after the moon landing had been successful.

"Landing a man on the moon and bringing him back safely was Kennedy's dream. President Lyndon Baines Johnson wasn't satisfied with simply making JFK's dream a reality. He wanted to be remembered for something other than the Vietnam War and seeding the moon with life would be hard to beat. He saw it as his chance to get his own *Eternal Flame* in the Arlington National Cemetery.

"For some reason, which remains unclear, the government decided the participants in the project be divided into ten isolated groups of two scientists each and assigned to Dr. Peter Langstrum, who reported to the project leader Dr. Mark Todd.

"My grandmother, Dr. Diane Walters, and Dr. Harry Robinson were assigned to one team, and I grew up reading about the Robinson/Walters team through my grandmother's personal diary.

"Some, but not all of her notes were included in the official *Ladder Project* dossier that I was able to study after being employed by the CIA a few weeks ago. Mostly, those notes were of a personal nature, such as her feelings and assumptions surrounding their work as their part of the project progressed.

"In these notes, she describes how Dr. Robinson always harbored doubts that the work of their team had much to do with the creation of a lunar life form.

"You see, Dr. Robinson had a sibling who died from a terrible genetic disease, and I believe his enthusiasm for gene research was the main reason he sought out a career in molecular biology.

"Robinson was obsessed with the *Cambrian Explosion* that occurred some 541 million years ago and lasted for over 20 million years, which resulted in modern metazoan phyla —— the emergence of animals into the ecosystem, and later, the scientific study of the theory of evolution.

"Evolution happens when there is damage to a cell, which causes the cell to alter its DNA structure in order to survive. If the damage is non-lethal, the cell can pass the altered gene along to its offspring.

"When viruses actually came to be is unclear, however, we do know that there are over 200 that have been found to infect humans. Most are harmless but their purpose seems to be to inject their own DNA into human cells and use the cell's replication machinery to create more copies of itself, when that happens as the cell struggles to survive it attempts to evolve before it is destroyed and releases additional viruses into our system. Viruses create evolution.

"Initially the virus drills a hole through the cell's membrane to gain entrance, but without the proper tool to do that, the virus dies. *Gain of function research* involves scientists providing the virus with a spear made of protein to pierce the wall of the cell that was not provided to the cell in nature. Their reason is to prepare for the chance the virus should develop the spear on its own. What would happen if, so-to-speak?

"I believe that Bong Hwa is trying to engineer a virus that causes humans to become nothing more than serfs so the government can go about its work without fear of interference. But he lacks the technology to make it infectious.

"The Chinese, through gain of function research, have been experimenting with Coronaviruses since SARS in 2003, and with MERS in 2013, and Bong Hwa has been writing letters to an unidentified Chinese lab technician to have his homemade virus included in their next Coronavirus event.

"Most researchers believe that evolution in humans ceased some forty-thousand years ago and another *Cambrian Explosion* is long overdue. Of those, many have expressed great fear of what another explosion might do to life on Earth and are researching ways to stop evolution permanently or at least get control of it. In my view, the cessation of evolution would prevent cells from adapting after being damaged by radiation, a new virus, or other means we can't even imagine, and the existence of our species would come to an end.

"I believe that the act of isolating Harry Robinson and my grandmother Diane from the other teams as they were, served as a playground for Robinson's fears that the main objective of *The Ladder Project* was to end evolution to stem world population growth.

"When my grandmother discovered Robinson had hung himself the morning after it was announced that the twenty-man research team would corroborate as a single, cohesive unit, she speculated something must have happened at that meeting that drove him over the edge.

"In her notes, she mentioned several weeks prior, when Robinson had continued to fail at inserting a simple gene into a single cell organism, mumbling to himself about 'identical locks having different keys', at their meeting she had overheard a Dr. Paul Simmons of a different team indicate he believed that he had solved part of that problem and wanted to set up a meeting with Dr. Robinson to discuss his findings.

"Knowing that Simmons' team was concentrating on methods of controlling evolution, Dr. Robinson's suspicions had been vindicated, at least in his own mind. He was certain that he had become an unwitting participant in what he feared the most...that he possessed the information that Simmons needed to complete his goal of stopping evolution permanently, and his choice would be to reveal his information to Simmons or not. He obviously could not withstand the pressure and decided suicide was his only out.

"Mr. Chairman, do you remember SARS, the first Coronavirus?"

"*Severe Acute Respiratory Syndrome.* It occurred in 2003, as

I recall. A virus identified by the Chinese that originated in bats. Spread mostly through air travel," the Chairman recited it as if he had been involved in a recent conversation regarding that very issue.

"You may also recall it caused a huge scare in the medical community," Anna May went on. "A member of the Coronaviridae family, it was projected to have a 3% infection rate, yet worldwide only around 8,000 people were infected and less than 10% of them died from it.

"The next coronavirus event was called MERS short for *Middle East respiratory syndrome* and appeared six years ago. Milder than SARS but transmitted from human-to-human contact faster than SARS. That coronavirus event's infection rate was forecasted at around 33%. It was isolated in the Middle East where it got its name, and less than 2,300 cases were confirmed and only about 800 died. There has been some speculation that the virus was created in a lab through 'gain of function research' but has been fiercely denied by the *World Health Organization* and the *People's Republic of China.*"

"Ms. Lee, do you believe these viruses were created in a lab and purposely introduced into the world?" the Chairman inquired.

"I'm not certain of SARS, but I am certain that MERS was a human creation," Anna May replied. "As sure as I am that a third event is being created as we speak. And I think this third event may be far worse than the previous two."

"Why are you so sure there will be another attempt?" the Chairman asked. "If someone were trying to kill us, Ms. Lee, they could have infected the world with Ebola and be done with it, wouldn't they?" the Chairman offered.

"Mr. Chairman, I don't think they are trying to kill us, as

you said. The answer is a bit more complicated, but it's the only thing that fits," Anna May continued. "There are studies going on that suggest coronavirus is the perfect messenger for slipping genetic material into human chromosomes. That's why it keeps showing up. Immunologists are not trying to kill coronaviruses. They want to use them to alter human DNA. By eliminating them, they become useless, but developing 'herd immunity' gives them the chance to mutate through natural causes."

"And do what?" the Chairman asked.

"Sooner or later, a coronavirus may come along that will be the one they're waiting for."

"Waiting for?" the Chairman sat erect in his chair.

"Mr. Chairman," Anna May continued, "scientists around the world are fascinated with coronaviruses. The President of the United States has already been warned that a new pandemic will occur within the next two years, and we are not prepared for it. There are hundreds if not thousands of these Kim Bong Hwa characters out there and I am more than a little concerned about what they are doing?"

"Dr. Blankin, do you know what the hell she is talking about?" the Chairman directed his question to one of the other members of the group.

Dr. Frank Blankin, a molecular biologist, bald-headed, and about fifty years of age, responded. "There has been some speculation along those lines, Mr. Chairman, but as far as I am aware, it's merely speculation."

The Chairman redirected his attention to Anna May. "If this is true, Ms. Lee, why don't we hear more about it?"

"Public opinion," Anna May responded. "As far back as 1978, under pressure, Congress attempted to bring all industrial research and development around the subject of gene-splicing under Federal regulation.

"Environmentalists, mainly an organization spearheaded by 'Friends of the Earth' aided by a Democrat Congressman, believed what they called 'gene-splicing' was too dangerous. As a result, at the request of the government, the public knows little about the subject, and the media has been instructed to keep it that way. In short, it was farmed out to the Chinese.

"Mr. Chairman," Anna May continued, "some molecular biologists are seriously pursuing this research, and if Kim Bong Hwa has been successful in altering the DNA of some of his victims in the North Korean prison camps and using coronaviruses as a delivery mechanism, it suggests he believes he can alter the DNA of every human being on the planet. All he lacks is an efficient delivery system, and something to control the timing. His friends in Beijing have the delivery system he needs. These coronavirus events will continue to be explored, and if they aren't stopped, there may be no one left on this planet to stop them.

"I think Bong Hwa believes he can alter the world's human DNA by *piggy-backing* genetic material into human chromosomes and utilize the Chinese government's distribution network which will satisfy their combined desires to take control of the Earth's population, killing billions of people in the process and shut down evolution through a new coronavirus event."

"So, what you're suggesting, Ms. Lee, is the most recent coronavirus events were not so much about the disease, as they were tests to discover how to remotely alter the DNA of the hosts?"

"And then grossly reducing the population to keep it that way," she added. "That's why Harry Swanson took his own life in 1967. He knew what it would take to stop evolution, and in his state of mind, he couldn't live with being the one to make it possible."

Anna Mae stayed on with the CIA. Bong Hwa remained in a prison in South Korea. North Korea demanded he be repatriated back to his homeland. South Korea responded with a statement that they never heard of Kim Bong Hwa and suggested they look in one of their other camps.

Epilogue

While this story is one of the author's imagination, it is based on the reality of what might have occurred in our past. The story does not end here. The Coronavirus has changed life on Earth as surely as the Cambrian Explosion made evolution possible. The effects caused by COVID-19 (the 3rd Event) is evidence of an on-going battle in man's determination to open one Pandora Box after another. In our attempts to lessen the effects of one Coronavirus event, are we inadvertently insuring the creation of another, more terrible one?

Coronavirus is everywhere. They are above or heads in bats and under our feet in rodents, and geneticists find them irresistible.

The jump from animal to human could have happened naturally, but *gain of function research* in a lab in Wuhan, China could have provided a faster solution.

From a recent article found at NPR.org, written by Michaeleen Doucleff PhD, she tells a chilling story and I paraphrase here:

As recently as March 2021, scientists claimed to have studied 24 new coronaviruses including four closely related to the virus that causes COVID-19, or SARS-CoV-2, and three viruses closely related to SARS-CoV, which caused a smaller outbreak back in 2003, and that's only the beginning.

There are literally thousands of coronaviruses throughout the world and they aren't limited to bats. Dogs, cats, birds, chickens, pigs and rodents also carry coronaviruses.

In the same article, Dr Edward Holmes at the University of Sidney was quoted as saying:

"I think we need to face reality here," Holmes says. "Coronavirus pandemics are not a once in a hundred-year events. "The next one could come at any time. It could come in fifty years or in ten years. Or it could be next year."

We are definitely not prepared.

* * *

Don't miss out on your next favorite book!
Join the Melange Books mailing list at
www.melange-books.com/mail.html

THANK YOU FOR READING

Did you enjoy this book?

We invite you to leave a review at the website of your choice, such as Goodreads, Amazon, Barnes & Noble, etc.

DID YOU KNOW THAT LEAVING A REVIEW...

- Helps other readers find books they may enjoy.
- Gives you a chance to let your voice be heard.
- Gives authors recognition for their hard work.
- Doesn't have to be long. A sentence or two about why you liked the book will do.

About the Author

Starting in 1978, Bill Scott has published several non-fictional books as well as fictional works, and several hundred articles and YouTube videos. Bill is currently the President of StoreReport LLC, which provides computers, software and cloud services to unique convenience store retailers and other similar types of retailers for over 44 years. Bill was born and raised in Shreveport Louisiana, served in the USAF in the early sixties after which he had several rock bands and traveled the US. During that time, before he started his successful computer business, Bill spent the majority of his time working in radio, television and print advertising.

Bill got into novels while writing operating manuals for his computer products. One night he had a dream that resulted in him being compelled to putting it all down on paper. Bill was tired of reading the same old stories over and over again filled with horror, crime, and sensationalism, so Bill enjoys producing material that causes people to think outside the box, wanting not merely to make his readers think, but to actually get them involved with his characters.

BillScott@StoreReport.com